California Bloodli

John Harvey is a prolific write
writes children's fiction and pc
magazine of writing and photography called *Slow Dancer*. At present he is doing research and a little teaching in the American Studies department of Nottingham University. He likes watching movies and one or two other things.

In the same series

Hart One: Cherokee Outlet
Hart Two: Blood Trail
Hart Three: Tago
Hart Four: The Silver Lie
Hart Five: Blood on the Border
Hart Six: Ride the Wide Country
Hart Seven: Arkansas Breakout
Hart Eight: John Wesley Hardin

John B. Harvey

Hart Nine:
California Bloodlines

Pan Original
Pan Books London and Sydney

First published 1981 by Pan Books Ltd.
Cavaye Place. London SW10 9PG

ISBN 0 330 26767 1
Typeset by Input Typesetting Ltd. London SW19 8DR
Printed and bound in Great Britain by Collins. Glasgow

for Julie:
sooner or later,
one of us must know . . .

One

The coffee was grey and lukewarm, tasted of beans that had been used too many times. Hart swished it round inside his mouth, trying to clear the stale taste of sleep and last night's whisky. He threw what remained in the cup wide to his right, stood up and lifted the enamel pot from the side of the fire. When the grounds sprayed across it, the fire sizzled up in abrupt yellow and purple flames. Hart shook the pot a few more times before pushing it down into one of the saddle bags which lay on the ground.

The grey mare stood patiently as he slipped on the bridle, patting her warm, broad nose. When he dropped the blanket onto her back, she turned her head and nudged him playfully and he raised his hand, pretending anger – a game they played often. Finally, as he tightened the cinch beneath the saddle flap, she snickered nervously and he patted her again and said softly: 'I know. I know. I seen 'em.'

The two riders made their way slowly along the southern side of the ridge, zigzagging through the cottonwoods. They rode without bothering to disguise their approach, single file, no more than ten yards between them. Hart recognized the leader from the previous night, a five-handed poker game with low stakes and little enough urgency. The man's name was Cantrell and he owned a small spread in the Rio Lobo valley fifteen miles to the west. There had been some desultory talk of offering Hart a job of work, but the rancher hadn't been sure if he was serious or not and Hart hadn't really wanted to go back to herding cattle and breaking broncs so it had petered out to nothing.

It had been one of those evenings.

' 'Lo, there!' The rancher raised his hand in greeting and led his mount off the ridge and down an easy diagonal towards where Hart had made his camp.

Hart acknowledged the greeting and carried on with his

business, tying the saddle bags back on the Denver saddle, kicking dirt over the remaining embers of the fire.

'Better'n a room in town,' said Cantrell pleasantly.

'Cheaper,' said Hart, his eyes shifting from the rancher to the man who rode behind him. He was younger than Cantrell by maybe ten, fifteen years. The left side of his face was somehow pulled down, the skin stretched tight over the bone and puckering in at the corner of his mouth in a pink scar. He held the reins loose around his right hand and the left never strayed far from the pistol that was holstered at his side.

Hart noticed that the small safety loop had been flicked back from around the hammer. Could be no more than he was a cautious man.

'This here's Bennett,' said Cantrell, glancing over his shoulder.

Hart nodded in the man's direction and Bennett flipped his right hand up towards his hat brim. The sorrel he was riding trotted a few paces, unsettled by the hasty movement of the rein.

'Looks like we're too late for coffee,' said Cantrell with a glance at the smouldering fire.

'You didn't miss much,' said Hart with a shrug.

The rancher hesitated, uncertain whether to move on or stay and talk. Hart sensed the uneasiness in him and wondered if it had anything to do with Bennett, whose hand was still fidgeting with the air not far above the grip of his gun.

'Seems last night,' Cantrell began, shifting his weight in the saddle, 'we was talkin' 'bout you comin' out to the ranch. Maybe workin' a spell.'

'We talked some.'

'You still feel that way?'

'I didn't say nothin' for sure.'

'I know an' I ain't fixin' to hold you to . . .'

'All the same with you, I'll let it pass. It's not that I ain't grateful, only . . . I ain't sure 'bout goin' back to ranch work.'

'Not when you can earn more money with a gun,' broke

in Bennett, his sorrel shifting sideways so that the angle between Bennett and Cantrell was wider and more difficult for Hart to cover. He wondered if it had been done on purpose and there wasn't any way of being sure.

Hart moved a pace back and faced Bennett more or less square. 'I worked with a gun, yeah.'

'Kinda good, too,' said Bennett grudgingly, the scarred side of his mouth twisting inwards as he spoke.

Hart shrugged, non-commital.

Bennett's mount edged a yard or so back in the other direction and tossed its head. 'Folk say you're a man as likes his work.'

Hart nodded: 'Man don't do that, what's he doin' it for?'

'Not everyone has that kind of choice,' put in Cantrell.

'Not everyone likes killin',' said Bennett, his voice taking on an edge that cut hard across the morning.

Light was lifting through the trees and the birds were at full-throat. A blue jay chased through the air and landed for no more than a moment on the ground between the two mounted men. Hart wondered whether Bennett was harbouring some kind of grudge against himself in particular or if it was no more than his way.

'You're right,' Hart said, 'No man likes killin'. Not without good reason.'

'That weren't what I said.'

'It'll do.'

Cantrell looked as if he was ready to turn his horse back up towards the trail, but Bennett held his ground, tightening the grip on his reins by giving them another turn around his wrist.

'You said it yourself,' Bennett said after a few seconds, 'man makes a choice. You made yours. You hire that fancy gun.'

He nodded towards the pearl-handled Colt Peacemaker holstered at Hart's side, the design of an eagle and snake clear upon the grip.

Hart willed his body to relax, falling into a slight crouch.

His eyes narrowed and his arm arched. Cantrell read the signs clearly enough and half-turned his mount away, called for Bennett to follow.

But Bennett stood his ground.

'I ain't crossed you before?' asked Hart.

Bennett shook his head.

'Your kin?'

'No.'

'Then either you better spit out what it is that's gripin' at your craw, or ride on out.'

'What puts you in mind you can give orders?' Bennett's voice was harder, shriller.

The blue jay seized on the rising tone and mimicked it back.

'Seems to me like you're gettin' awful pushy for a feller without reason. Either that, or there's things you're holdin' back.'

'That wouldn't be sayin' I'm a liar, would it?'

'An' you wouldn't be edgin' me into a fight just so's maybe you can get yourself a reputation?'

Bennett threw back his head and laughted aloud, blackened stumps of teeth showing clear. 'Reputation? For takin' trash like you?'

Hart's body swayed almost imperceptibly and his fingers grazed the mother-of-pearl of his Colt. The faded blue of his eyes gripped Bennett and held him fast. 'Reputation or not, you let that hand of yours toy with that gun five seconds longer and I'm goin' to have to blow you out the saddle!'

Bennett's face twisted and his mouth sucked in the pink of his scar. But there was sweat standing out clear now on his forehead and the fingers of his hand closed into a fist and lifted slowly away from his holster.

'Come on!' called Cantrell. 'We got time to make up.'

Bennett's tongue pushed between his lips and wet them nervously, like a snake. The fist rested on the curved pommel of his saddle and he continued to stare at Hart but now both of them knew it was over and all that was happening was that he was saving as much face as he could.

Cantrell raised a hand towards Hart and set his mount to climb back towards the line of cottonwoods. Bennett backed his horse away and then swung its head violently, kicking hard into its flanks with spurred boots. Hart turned and straightened, watching the two men as they hit the ridge, watching them until they were almost out of sight. Hart felt the tenseness begin to clear from his body and slowly he uncurled the fingers of his gun hand, the centre of his palm dry as bone, the skin around it damp with sweat.

He was already remembering a time back in Indian Territory when he'd been crossing the street of a place no bigger than a dozen ramshackle buildings and as many tents. He'd been talking in the general store that served as a saloon, swapping yarns with a couple of old-timers and recalling days down in Arizona when he'd been pretty wild and wearing the badge of a deputy marshall in Tucson.

The evening had drifted to some kind of an ending the way those kind of evenings do and Hart had bade everyone goodnight and set off towards the barn where he'd stabled his horse and was intending to throw down his bed roll in the hay.

The street was pretty dark, just the dim light from the kerosene lamp that hung from the ceiling of the store and a vague glow from the canvas of a few tents. He'd heard footsteps behind him and thought nothing special of them – no cause for alarm, simply someone else seeking some place to stretch out and wait for morning.

It was the voice that did it: high, edgy, a shriek that cut through the stillness like a night bird's wing.

'Draw, you bastard!'

He'd spun fast, body ducking, swerving low as he moved left to right. His arm, hand, fingers – all had worked as fast, as smoothly as they were trained. Worked without conscious thought. The hammer had come back, the triple click clear in the almost deserted street. The man facing him with his back to the door of the general store not more than a dark shape, a glint of metal for an instant at his side.

Hart's first shot had sent him staggering backwards, five, six faltering paces that lodged him against the uneven boards of the store wall. The second bullet had burst his left side apart, splintering the ribs above the heart.

Voices, loud and fast, feet running on boards, and then it was the lamp swinging above the store owner's head, edges of its shadow shifting back and forth over the slumped body.

Man! Hart's stomach had knotted when he gazed down at the face for the first time. He was little more than a kid. Fifteen. Sixteen at most. The first few fair hairs curling from his soft, slack jaw. Blood splattering his cheek.

Hart watched as one of the bystanders bent down and lifted the old Colt Navy from where it lay, some dozen feet from the boy's spread hand.

Hart's guts turned, cold.

Questions and accusations rose about him and he could do nothing but stand and stare down. Not for minutes, and then he gulped air into his lungs and slid the Colt down into its holster and turned away. He'd never seen the kid before in his life, hadn't seen him then, not properly – just a shadowy shape coming at him out of the dark with a gun in his hand and a threat on his lips.

'Draw, you bastard!'

And that was what Hart had done.

And the kid who'd been out to make a name for himself, who'd squatted down outside the store earlier that night, even hovered around the edges of the small crowd and heard the tales about guns and death down near the Arizona border, had sneaked home and found the gun some kinfolk had likely used in the War Between the States and pushed it down into his belt like a real gunfighter.

Fifteen and growing up in a shanty in the middle of Indian Territory, no way out except you made yourself special, got noticed, acquired a reputation. But it came harder than that unless you were born lucky. And that kid laying back there propped up against the wall with blood leaking from his already dead body, he hadn't been born lucky at all. Maybe, best if he'd never been born at all. In the morning that followed, Hart had risen and walked early into a northerly wind and dared the sullen and accusing eyes of the kid's family while he tossed down ten dollars to pay for his burial. Knowing as he did so that the father would carry the boy out towards the foothills on the back of a mule and dig a deep hole himself, throw the body down and finally set stones over the covered earth to keep the coyotes and wolves away from his son's bones. The ten dollars would be spent on food and corn liquor and maybe some nails or rope and they'd be well spent. Whatever they went on, they wouldn't go any way towards helping Hart forget what he'd done, nor the first shock of seeing the kid's face as it came out of shadow into the swing of light.

That was Bennett's answer if he'd ever wanted to hear it, which of course he hadn't. Killing didn't come easy to a man like Hart – easy in the doing, all right, but not more than that. Sure, there'd been men enough at the raw end of his guns who'd needing killing. Hart hadn't been sorry for their deaths but neither had he enjoyed it. It had been something to be done, more often than not something he had been paid to do and on occasion he'd been wearing a lawman's badge and on others he had not but that hadn't mattered at all.

Then there'd been those like the kid in that dark street whose deaths haunted him, waiting for the least chance to filter back towards the front of his mind. Blood and broken bone and life shot out.

Hart's thoughts shifted for a moment, far back beyond Indian Territory, back beyond Tuscon to when he was no more than fourteen himself and leaving home. Three sisters and a brother, the brother not yet four years old. Hart hadn't thought of him in years.

If he'd lived Sean would be in his twenties, farming somewhere, prospecting like his father, Hart's own step-father. In his twenties if he hadn't stepped out in some dirty, dark street with a gun clutched heavy in his hand and words on his lips that would bring some stranger spinning round . . .

Hart slotted his boot into the stirrup and pulled himself up into the saddle. Cantrell and Bennett had had plenty of time to get a good start down the trail that he too was going to follow. The sun was beginning to break and the day was his own. He'd let the grey take her own time and watch the land slowly change as he rode west, waiting for the first signs of snow on the far hills.

Two

At roughly the same time that Wes Hart was tracking Cantrell and Bennett along the cottonwood ridge, R. G. Fowler was lurching from sleep and hurling back a sprawl of sweat-sodden clothes in an urgent need to get his feet to the floor. The shock of impact jarred him and he set both hands to the sides of his burly head and groaned. Despite the discomfort he swayed to his feet and started to negotiate his way, bleary-eyed, across the room. A stack of fliers and magazines went flying as he struck it with a flailing arm; a pile of law books stuttered as he floundered past and two volumes upended themselves onto a plate thickly coated with congealed gravy flecked grey with cigar ash.

He had to piss even though taking a piss caused him considerable discomfort, even though the releasing of the deep yellow fluid made him wince and grit his teeth and rock backward and forward above the rising steam.

Fowler groaned with a mixture of consternation and delight and fingered himself sloppily back into his long johns, ignoring the fresh pee stain which was spreading in a loose circular shape over the others. He shook his pudgy fingers and wiped them down the sides of his vest, cleared his throat, spat down into the steadying swirl of piss at the bottom of the brimming chamberpot, and stumbled to the window.

Three shots of fresh air and he closed it again and reached over for the bottle and uncorked his breakfast.

In less than half an hour Fowler had dressed himself in the least shabby of his two dark suits, that with only one cigar burn on the vest and without frayed cuffs. His shirt was creased but clean and there was a perfunctory shine on his boots from where he'd brushed them up against the backs of his suit pants while leaning against the wardrobe. His dark, thinning hair looked, rightly, as if he'd managed to poke his fingers through it and rid it of the worst of the tangles; his beard and moustache – also dark but lighter, almost ginger, about the mouth – were less unkempt than was usually the case and free from traces of food for the sole reason it had been some time since Fowler had sullied his stomach with solids.

The left side of the suit jacket bulged somewhat on account of the shoulder rig that his fingers had succeeded in securing at the third, or was it the fourth, attempt. A Smith and Wesson .44, its barrel shortened from the regulation six and a half inches to five, sat snug in the holster, hammer resting on an empty chamber.

Fowler had woken once in the middle of the night with a start, sure that someone had come into the room where he'd fallen asleep on the floor with his street clothes still on and smeared with vomit. In his urgency, he'd grabbed the .44 and come very close to shooting off his left foot.

Ever since that time he'd vowed always to remain conscious till he'd removed his holster and had been careful to slip no more than five shells into the chamber.

At the front door he shrugged his bear-like shoulders round

and growled so viciously at his landlady's request for some rent money that she retreated as fast as she could behind her parlour door and worked at her sampler as quickly as her swollen and arthritic fingers would allow.

Fowler stood for a few minutes on the sidewalk and looked up and down the tree-lined street and decided for the fifth time in the past five days that he was as sick of Sacramento as a jelly roll stud who'd fallen through the roof of a whore-house and couldn't get back out.

He sniffed at the air and found it treacherous enough to merit a shot more bourbon. The silver flask came out of his hip pocket almost as fast as another man would draw a pistol. Thing was, the bourbon took a deal longer to stretch a man out and was a sight more pleasurable in the process.

He walked towards the livery stable with all the assurance of a man whose mind is toying with the idea that the earth is liable to crack apart at any moment. Which, since he was in California, was not quite as fanciful as it might seem.

Mrs MacPhail lived in the foothills of the Sierras, about an hour's ride north-east of Spanish Flat. Fowler had quarrelled with the office, demanding that his client, if that was what she was to be, should get in one of the several fancy carriages she obviously owned and get herself driven down to Sacramento. But his argument carried no weight with the Old Man, who was too pleased with the prospect of some of the MacPhail gold coming his way to pay heed to the likes of Fowler.

Indeed, he was loath to send someone as disreputable as Fowler at all but all of the other operatives were out of town on other work and the only alternative would have been to have made the journey himself.

He didn't want the gold in his safe that much.

So it was Fowler who sat heavy in the saddle of his placid chestnut mare and took the Green Valley road to the American River, sweated and cursed up the Marshall Grade until he levelled out on the Black Oak Mine road and was all set for Spanish Flat.

Well, he should have been set, anyway. But other things intervened, like the mare taking a stone in her back shoe and Fowler getting a powerful thirst that his flask couldn't handle. He had no sooner wiped the dirt from the knees of his suit after dealing with the horse's stone than he remembered there was a little general store up into the hills to the north of Black Oak Road. It sold about every damn thing you could think of, from hard tack to nails, and at times a man could be excused for thinking he'd paid for one and come away with the other. But what mattered to Fowler was that the place also sold liquor.

He managed to make his way up the winding track, ducking under low branches that sought to unseat him, and succeeded in tearing a rent several inches wide across the centre of his coat back. Insects swarmed about his face and lashing out at them angrily he bloodied his knuckles against a tree close enough to meet the end of his swing. By the time he'd convinced himself that he'd taken the wrong track – or that the store had been a figment of his drunken imagination – there it was. Built out from the hillside so that the earth formed the back wall and part of the roof, it was fashioned from all manner of planks and boards and packing cases, patched here and there with tin. A mule was tied up outside and gazed at Fowler forlornly before depositing a giant turd as a form of greeting. A black and white goat, attached to a stake, sat on the roof and bleated.

Fowler tethered his horse out of range of the mule and pushed open the door.

The interior was dark and musty and smelt of rancid goats' cheese and corn liquor and a few other things Fowler likely could have identified if he'd worked at it. Instead he nodded briefly at the couple of farmers who were taking a drink at the only table, set a squat hand on the greasy counter and asked the one-eyed man back of it for a shot of bourbon.

When it came it was in a glass that was chipped in several places round the edge as if one of the previous customers had tried to bite his way through the rim. The contents bore about as much resemblance to bourbon as a Nogales whore to a convent nun. Fowler drank it with his eyes more or less shut and his breath clemmed up in his throat. It still didn't taste any better.

He wiped the back of his grazed hand across his mouth and put the glass back down with a bang. 'Sure that's bourbon?'

'What it says on the label.'

'Put up a sign out front callin' this the Excelsior Palace, still wouldn't be no more'n a flea-bitten old shack stinkin' of goat shit!'

The one-eyed man stood back from the bar a-ways and set his head to one side. 'Shouldn't say things like that, mister. 'T'ain't nice. Specially from strangers.'

Fowler nodded. He was hot and thirsty and riding up the Grade hadn't helped his temper. At the end of it all he'd likely spend ten minutes with some rich old woman who'd give him orders like he was a kid with dirt hangin' out of his ears and send him on his way without so much as a drink. He leaned a little towards the man and said in his growl of a voice: 'Tell you what you do, you throw some lamp oil about the place an' hand me a match. That's about the only way you'll clean this hole up and make it fit for callers. You understand me?'

One-Eye scratched at a red sore at the side of his neck, close by a jutting angle of bone. His fingers were long and ingrained with dirt, their nails cracked and jagged. His single eye was large and dark and watery, a sliver of deep yellow passing over the top of the pupil. As Fowler stared at it, the eye twitched.

'Got scratched an' stung all the hell comin' up here,' Fowler went on, warming to his subject, letting all of his anger and frustration well out. 'All for what? A shot of somethin' out of a bottle with a bourbon label stuck on it which you get filled by lettin' that mule of yours out there piss in it!'

'Hey, mister!' called one of the farmers off to the side. 'That's my mule you're talkin' about.'

'You shut your damned mouth!' burst Fowler, swinging him a threatening look. 'This ain't none of your concern.'

'I told you, that's my mule.' He stood up and it took him a long time before he stopped. He wasn't slow, just tall. Very tall. With his black hat crammed right down on his head, he was too tall for that room by a good twelve inches.

Fowler shrugged his heavy shoulders and turned away. The feller behind the bar was still looking put out and he showed a few broken ends of tooth in an otherwise empty mouth. Fowler wasn't sure if the man was about to say something or spit.

Either way, Fowler moved to one side and slid his hand over the counter pretty quick, palming the quarter he'd paid for the drink.

The single, watering eye stared at him astonished. 'Mister, you can't . . .'

'Just did,' Fowler informed him, and he tipped the coin down into the side pocket of his torn coat.

'That's robbery.'

'If that's robbery, what d'you call chargin' a quarter for that rotten mule's-piss you call bourbon?'

'I told you afore, stranger,' called the farmer, his head jammed up against the ceiling, 'don't you go bad-mouthin' my mule.'

'An' I told you to shut your mouth!'

Fowler scowled at him and his partner and headed for the door.

'Mister!'

Fowler shook his head and kept on walking. The farmer was beginning to move across towards him and he glanced round and looked to see if he was carrying a gun. Which he wasn't.

One-Eye was.

He'd pulled it out from where it lay inside an old biscuit box under the counter and now he was holding it at arm's length, the long barrel pointing towards Fowler's back.

'Mister, you come back here with my money!'

'Jesus Christ!' shouted Fowler, turning just before the doorway. 'How many times I got to explain . . .'

Then he saw the pistol and knew that the time for explaining had run out. As the man's bony finger started to pull back on the trigger, Fowler decided to take evasive action. He threw himself sideways as quick as he could, his burly body hammering into a couple of flour sacks and driving them into a crate of assorted nails and a pile of boots and shoes, none of which matched. The moment he hit the floor the gun exploded and a bullet tore away a section of the roof a couple of feet from the top of the door.

Fowler shook his head, breathing with difficulty. His elbow stung where it had struck the floor and his forearm was numb. He made the mistake of taking his weight on that arm and toppled forward, butting one of the flour sacks. Over his shoulder he could see the one-eyed man struggling with the hammer of the long-barrelled gun. He shifted his weight onto his other arm and started to reach inside his jacket for the Smith and Wesson. The stubbed ends of his fingers had just passed between coat and shirt when the tall farmer kicked him in the chest, the toe of his boot landing immediately below Fowler's arm.

He was shunted several feet backwards, mouth open to a roar of surprise and pain, hand still half inside his coat. The farmer laughed and advanced on him, swinging his leg back to take a kick that sought to take his head clean off his body.

At that moment One-Eye succeeded in releasing the hammer of his gun and the slug ripped through the side of the farmer's throat and embedded itself in the front wall. Blood spurted up over the ceiling, down the wall and across the floor. The farmer's hands were at his throat, clapped over the wound as if trying to hold the torn flesh together. Blood seeped between his fingers and dribbled down his arms.

His friend ran towards him, stopped when he saw the extent of the wound, the amount of blood.

One-Eye now had the pistol in both hands but it was pointed down towards the top of the counter and slowly sliding forward through his long fingers.

A loud gurgling sound came from the farmer, but not from his mouth.

The man back of him cursed and turned away, one hand to his mouth to catch the vomit.

Fowler managed to get to his feet and to clear his Smith and Wesson from his holster. He approached the bar side-on and took the gun from One-Eye's hands without the least resistance. He thought about pushing it down into his belt but didn't want to blow his balls off so he ended up hurling it through the door.

The wounded man pitched forward until his forehead was resting on the scarred boards and the blood was running freely down both sides of his face, curling, some of it, into his nose and eyes. His hands fell away from the back of his neck and smeared the floor.

The sound of his partner's vomiting was loud in the enclosed space.

Fowler waited until the retching had stopped and pulled the man over the table and made him sit down. He forced a glass of corn liquor down his throat so that the tears sprang to his eyes. He asked him his name and that of the dying farmer. The feeling returning to his arm so that the blood tingled and itched like crazy, Fowler wrote out an account of what had happened, using a stub of pencil in the front of the notebook the Old Man insisted he carry but which he hardly ever used.

When he'd done that he read it to the man at the table and to One-Eye, taking the words clear and slow like he would have done talking to a child or an idiot. All the while, the farmer's throat was gurgling air and spluttering blood through the wound at its back.

Fowler got the two men to make their marks at the bottom of the paper, though he doubted if either of them had really understood what he'd written or what they were doing.

Fowler looked at the farmer, whose long body was now stretched across the flour sacks, the front of his work overalls deep with blood. The building stank of blood and vomit now, to accompany the smell of goats' cheese and liquor. He reached over the bar for the bottle labelled bourbon and took a swig from the neck, washing it quickly around his mouth before spitting it out without swallowing a drop.

Outside, his chestnut mare looked at him questioningly and he gave her some water in an old bucket before mounting up and riding out. Half-way down the track he looked back and could only see one small section of the ramshackle wall. He wondered if the farmer had managed to die yet, whether the other two were in a strong enough state to bury him before stiffness set in and they would have to break his long limbs to fit him into the ground.

Three

There were two envelopes waiting for Wes Hart in the postal office at Virginia City. One had been there a month and the other no more than two days; both were held behind a criss-cross of coloured string back of the main counter. The clerk would keep them there for a six-month and, if no one had claimed them by that date, consign them to one of the drawers in the outer office. There they'd slowly begin to fade and yellow until their messages of hope or hate, love or greeting, would be illegible.

As it happened Hart had been in Virginia City the best part of a day without checking his mail. Since he could count on the fingers of both hands the number of letters he'd received in his entire life, that's hardly surprising. It had seemed more important to get his mare, Clay, stabled and tended to, find himself a room and stash away a few of his belongings, sit in the barber's chair alongside the plate glass window and watch the world go by while the beard was shaved clean from his chin and mouth, his lank hair was trimmed and hot rough towels were laid over his face.

Half an hour later and still smelling of the toilet water the barber had managed to splash onto his face unawares, Hart went into the first store he came to and bought two pairs of long socks in dark grey wool, a red vest, two cotton shirts – one plain green, dark rather than light, and one a brown and red check – a box of .44 cartridges which would serve for both his pistol and rifle. He mulled over buying some ten-gauge shot and finally decided against it.

The sign painted outside Hart's next stop was bright and confident: *Washng and Ironng – Hot Bath 10 cents*. He gave the contents of one saddle bag to the Chinaman behind the counter and asked for a bath. One Chinaman led to another and then another and finally Hart was led to a converted shed with a corrugated iron roof and four tall baths which were made in such a way that the customer sat up in them while alternating buckets of hot and cold water were poured over him by a fat Chinese who climbed unsteadily up and down a ladder resting on one of the old roof beams.

Hart pulled off the clothes he was wearing and gave instructions that the shirt, vest and socks be added to the pile he'd left out front at the laundry. Grudgingly, he got into the bath and waited for the fat man to pass him a cake of soap so large he could only just hold it in one hand.

As he washed himself he recalled a time when he'd taken a bath in a whorehouse and his back had been soaped and lathered by a beautiful girl with traces of Cree and Negro blood whose hands had been like butterflies. There'd been a bottle of good brandy within reach on the floor and she'd put a good cigar between his teeth and lit it for him, striking the match against the four-inch heel of her fashion shoe.

That had been back when he'd been good friends with Kate Stein and he'd acted as a trouble-shooter for her, keeping out the drunks and making sure that any complaints didn't come to blows. No one drew a weapon all the while Hart and Kate were together, their business relationship never quite straying over the line where it would have become personal. But Hart had ridden out from Creek City to clean up a place called Tago and when he finally got back Kate had sold out and gone and their business relationship was over. The place had been bought by a sanctimonious and tight-fisted Scot by the name of Kennedy who'd hired Hart to look after his daughter, Alice. After that things had got pretty complicated and the presence of a detective called Fowler hadn't helped. Well, at first it hadn't – but finally Fowler had dragged himself clear of his bourbon-haze long enough to throw in with a strong hand and the two of them had parted more or less friends.*

Hell, thought Hart as he towelled himself down, it all seems a long time back, a lot of towns ago. He dressed himself in his old denim pants and scuffed, plain boots, his new vest and the new green shirt; he threw the fat Chinaman a quarter and pushed his wide-brimmed, flat-crowned hat down onto his head. Out on the sidewalk he didn't look so much different from any other cowboy or wrangler that might be in town. Except there was something about the way his wiry, strongly muscled body moved – a sense of power under keen control, strength kept in check. His cheek bones were high and showed clearly against the tanned and now smooth skin of his lean face. The faded blue of his eyes told part of what he'd seen, understanding mingled with regret. He

* See Hart the Regulator 3 and 4, *Tago* and *The Silver Lie*.

walked with purpose, his right hand brushing the holster of his gun belt, fingers close to the mother-of-pearl grip of his Peacemaker.

When men came towards him on the boardwalk, it never occurred to Hart to step aside: it never occured to them to do anything else.

Hart glanced at a hay wagon moving slowly down the centre of the street, drawn by a team of four mules and driven by a kid who wasn't many months past his twelfth birthday. For an instant the thought of the son he'd never had tugged at him the way it sometimes did and as swiftly passed away again. He waited till the wagon had passed and crossed the street towards the nearest saloon. A quick shot of whisky broke the dust at the back of his throat and he was ordering another to chase down the first when both doors, front and back, opened at the same time.

Hart dropped the glass to the counter and his hand sped to his gun but the fingers froze around the butt.

Standing at the rear a heavy-bellied man cradled a shotgun over his arm like he meant business. The curled twin hammers were held back and the barrel ends angled up sufficiently to cut a deal of Hart into two where he stood. The other door was occupied by a tall man leaning his left hand on a walnut walking stick, most of his weight going with it. The other hand was filled with a Colt Frontier and the finger was tight against the trigger.

Both men had badges pinned to their vests.

Hart released his breath slowly and eased his hand clear of his pistol, stretching it on top of the bar, fingers spread wide.

'Clean him, Lefty', ordered the man with the stick.

The deputy lowered the hammers of the shotgun and held it in one hand while he used the other to pull Hart's gun from its holster, glance admiringly at the engraved handle, and tuck it down into the top of his pants.

'That all?'

Lefty felt Hart over with his free hand, failing to find the double-bladed knife that was pushed down in an Apache sheath inside his right boot.

'Turn around,' said the sheriff and Hart did as he was told, setting his back against the edge of the counter and watching as the lawman limped into the centre of the saloon.

Noises in the street told those inside that the news had already begun to spread and the usual collection of drunks and small boys and stray dogs would be on hand to watch what went down.

Those already inside the saloon edged away from any possible lines of fire, silent save for the excited scrape of their breathing, the rasp of their chairs across the uneven boards of the floor. The bartender shifted from one leg to the other nervously, worried about his glasses and stock, to say nothing of the new painted mirror shipped from St Louis.

Hart watched and waited, sensing that the sheriff was sizing him up, taking his time, enjoying his moment.

'Fancy gun,' commented the deputy.

Hart ignored him, watching the sheriff instead.

'How d'you feel 'bout walkin' down to the jail?' the lawman asked finally.

Hart stared at him for several seconds before answering. 'I got any choice?'

The sheriff almost smiled. 'Not a deal.'

Hart set his head to one side and nodded. 'You sure 'bout this?'

'Meanin' what?'

'You ain't confused me with someone else?'

'Why the hell should we do that?' asked the deputy with more than a trace of anger.

The sheriff shot him a quick glance that shut him up quicker than a jack rabbit bolting down his hole.

'I mean, you ain't arrestin' me or nothin', are you?' Hart asked.

'Any reason we should?'

'You mean you just bust in here flashin' guns that way for some kind of fun?'

The sheriff frowned, shifted his hold of the walnut stick. 'Don't get fresh with your lip!'

Hart held his tongue; there wasn't any sense to riling the man more than was necessary. Not without reason. It wasn't the first time some diligent peace officer had taken it into his head to remove his gun from him and breath a sight more easy. Quite a few had tried and some had even succeeded. The feller with the walnut stick was one of them and that gave him cause for a little respect in Hart's eyes anyway.

'I ain't arrestin' you,' the sheriff said, 'not yet anyways. We go down the office there's more time to check through them fliers as keep comin' by. Man can't hold 'em all to mind. You understand that?'

'Sure can.'

'You ever wear a badge?'

'Uh-huh.'

'Like hell he did!' put in the deputy.

'One of these times you open that mouth of yours too soon,' snapped the sheriff, 'you're gonna trip your foot in it an' finish up swallowin' your ass!'

The deputy smarted and shuffled his feet, looking away. Hart and the sheriff shared a laugh.

'When was this?' the lawman asked, the smile still on his face. 'The badge.'

'Few years back, over in Indian Territory. Rode as deputy US marshal for a time. Didn't take to it much.'

The sheriff thought a while. 'You'd be workin' with Fagan then?'

'Yeah.'

'Tough old bastard.' The sheriff laughed shortly and shook his head. 'Rode with him once ten or more years back. Posse chasin' after three fellers who held up the Overland stage, stole the mails, bust open the strongbox, shot an' killed the driver and the guard. We hounded them bastards best part of a week an' never come close enough to smell 'em. Fagan drove us hard as any man could, though.' He tapped his stick on the ground. 'That was before I stopped this.'

The deputy cleared his throat, aimed for the nearest spittoon and missed by a good six inches. Hart wondered if his gunplay was as accurate. The sheriff was through with reminiscing. He nodded towards the door and Hart headed towards it, walking slow so's not to give the deputy a chance to cut loose with his scattergun.

It took the best part of half an hour to run through the bundles of wanted notices that had accumulated in the desk drawers of the sheriff's office and none of them showed Hart to have a price on his head. He sat on a hard chair patient enough, swapping a few yarns with the lawman whenever a face or a name set some memory stalking.

He found out the sheriff's name was Herb Mosley and he'd been wearing one badge or other for the best part of twenty years. A couple of slugs from a Winchester had slowed him down some, left him with a stiff leg that played merry hell whenever it rained and made the sweat bust out if there was a storm. He'd taken on Zed Rawlings as deputy and while he'd never got to like him and didn't altogether trust his judgement, nobody better had come along.

Mosley said this while the deputy was out at the nearest saloon fetching a couple of beers. A look passed between the sheriff and Hart when he talked about not finding anybody better, just quick, no big thing, but enough for the question to be asked and answered and for the sheriff to shrug, as much to say he didn't altogether blame him.

They were half-way down the glass of beer when Hart leaned forward and asked to look at a poster one more time.

The drawing was kind of sketchy and the eyes weren't exactly right, yet . . .

'Know him?' asked the sheriff, getting to his feet and using his stick to hobble round behind Hart's chair.

'Could be.' Hart looked at the flier again, turning it this way and that, still not quite certain. 'Only he weren't callin' himself this, not Barlow. Feller I'm thinkin' of went under the name of Bennett.'

'That don't mean a thing.'

'I know it.'

'Man can change his name quicker'n his pants.'

'Specially if he's got reason enough.'

Mosley lifted the poster away from Hart and held it closer to his face so that he could read the print. He pronounced the words as he read them as if reading wasn't an activity he was well practised in.

'Wanted for armed robbery and murder. Together with High-Hat Thomas and Cherokee Dave Speedmore and three others unknown, on the fourteenth day of July, 1880, Henry George Barlow held up the Egan County Branch of the Nevada Mining Company Bank at Ely. Eight hundred dollars were stolen, one clerk beaten and seriously wounded and the manager shot and killed. Reward of three hundred dollars paid by the Nevada Mining Company Bank for the capture of Barlow. One tenth reward in addition from any money returned.'

Mosley slipped the paper back down to Hart and fetched his beer off the corner of the desk.

'Where d'you run across him? This Bennett?'

'Ridin' over Shoshone way, takin' the trail off of Railroad Pass out of Austin. He was ridin' with a rancher name of Cantrell. Me an' Cantrell we'd played a little cards together. He was lookin' to hire on a top hand. Asked me but I weren't interested.'

'You reckon this Bennett was fixin' to take the job?'

'Could be. Neither of 'em said. They was ridin' together, though. No doubt of that.'

The sheriff took some papers from his desk, a sack of tobacco from his vest pocket, and started, methodically, to roll himself a cigarette. 'What kind of a feller he strike you as bein'?'

'Quick-tempered son-of-a-bitch. Did his damndest to rile me into a fight.'

'No reason?'

'No. Never saw him before him an' Cantrell come ridin' up when I was breakin' camp.'

'He never figured you for a lawman or such?'

'That I don't know. I sure never give him no reason to think so.'

Mosley succeeded in lighting his cigarette at the second attempt. He lifted his stiff leg onto the edge of the desk with more difficulty than that, raked back his chair and sat enjoying his smoke for a while, leaving Hart to his own thoughts. The deputy came into the office from feeding the two prisoners locked in the cells, glanced round the silent room, lifted his shotgun down from the rack of the wall and went out.

With the sound of the door still echoing, Mosley said: 'Three hundred dollars ain't a bad pot of money for bringin' in one man.'

Hart just nodded, waiting.

'You pretty flush right now?'

'Bought some shirts an' a shave this morning' and I'm all but cleaned out.'

A smile settled on the sheriff's lined face. 'Well, now, ain't that somethin'.'

'You got jurisdiction over in Egan County?'

'I can get it.'

Hart nodded, easing himself out of the chair and standing close in front of the sheriff's broad desk. 'That deputy of yours, we don't . . .'

'Hell, no! He can stay an' look after the town. Sides, havin' him along'd only spoil the fun.'

Herb Mosley grinned and Hart kind of smiled and when they rode out of Virginia City at first light there were still two envelopes waiting for Hart back of the counter at the post office.

Four

Lydia MacPhail was forty-seven years old and weighed close on two hundred pounds. Her hair was brittle grey and so tightly curled that it gave the impression that a brisk stroke with a comb would chip pieces of it away. She tended to wear long, loose dresses in severe colours, usually modified by a faint pattern of checks or diagonal lines. These, like most things she bought, were brought direct to her door by a freight company working out of San Francisco. Some of her dresses originated in England, a good deal of her lingerie came from France. From time to time an outburst of extravagance overtook her and in this way she had acquired a number of statues of horses and dogs from Italy; all of these she had by now lost patience with and they were to be found scattered about the gardens that surrounded the house overlooking ridge after ridge of pines and cedars. She had also bought gilt mirrors which were now fixed to the four walls of her drawing room and which she liked to think (at those certain times when teasing herself in such a way was welcome) had spent the earlier years of their life in a New Orleans whorehouse.

MacPhail was the name she had taken when she had married her third husband, the one she chose to keep. She kept it, not because she remembered him (when she remembered him at all) with any particular fondness, but because it was also the name of her only son, Robert.

She had married first when little more than a girl and the rancher who came night after night to sit rocking on her father's porch astonished both of her parents by pausing late in the evening in the act of untying his horse from the hitching rail and asking if he could marry their daughter, Lydia. They were as surprised as they were partly because the rancher was almost the same age as themselves, partly as in all his visits he never seemed to have paid Lydia any attention. It was true that he'd not exchanged more than a couple of dozen words with her, but he had looked. Not long, not often, but enough. Lydia was not so much a girl that she had failed to understand the meaning of those passing, shifting glances of appraisal. When her startled parents went into the room where she was feigning sleep and informed her of the rancher's offer she was unable even to pretend surprise.

Her mother was of the opinion that Lydia should accept marriage as soon as any man of substance offered it, and the rancher was certainly that. Her father, though, soft of heart as fathers often are about their only daughter, had always argued that Lydia should make her own choice and marry for love. But Lydia knew she was not the kind of girl that most men considered pretty and sensed that the older she got the more this would be the case. She looked at the silhouette of the farmer pacing up and down alongside his patient horse, seeing him through the screen door illuminated for moments at a time by the fireflies that darted through the close night. She saw him and saw a way out of northern Montana.

Her father's surprise was compounded by her ready acceptance, her mother was delighted. The wedding had scarcely been consummated (with little pleasure for Lydia, yet little pain) when her husband was badly gored by a longhorn bull and spent five agonized weeks while the wound in his groin refused to respond to treatment and the colour and life gradually drained out of him.

Lydia nursed him efficiently and well, almost lovingly, and she was at his bedside when he wrote his will in weak, sprawling letters and left the ranch and its stock to her alone.

At the funeral she set up conversation with a banker who was a friend of her father's and inside another month the ranch had been sold to an absentee landlord who lived in Edinburgh and Lydia was on her way from Montana to California and her vision through the screen door proved finally correct.

She stayed aloof from men for the next few years, investing her money in land and a small shipping line and setting up a dress shop in the fashionable area of San Francisco which was so successful she soon owned two others which were managed by independently minded women like herself.

Lydia met Gerald MacPherson at a dinner party on Nob Hill, the weight of the silver on the table enough to sink one of her ships on its way south to the Cape. He was fresh from Scotland and inevitably the sale of her ranch was mentioned, and from then on MacPherson monopolized her completely. Not only that evening, but many others. He was seven years younger than her, handsome in a pretty and vacant sort of way, his manners were good and Lydia's inquiries into his finances showed that his family had given him a more than generous allowance to get him away from a scandal involving one of their servants.

He asked her early one morning, after they had danced close to exhaustion, if she would allow him to stay for what remained of the night in her bed. She patted his hand and told him that such things were allowable with serving girls but not with ladies. Gerald gave in and asked her to marry him. Lydia pretended to think about it for three days and then agreed. She took Gerald to her on their wedding night with a voraciousness that he never quite got over and which never was to be repeated.

After less than a year of marriage, gold fever struck and Gerald went into the city and bought an eighteen-inch-diameter gold pan, a pick and a long-pointed shovel, a crevice knife, a bucket, a magnet for removing black sand and a hand-lens and tweezers for tiny grains. He added a number of stoppered storage bottles and a set of scales, which the storekeeper suggested might be a touch optimistic.

He bought cooking utensils and a variety of foodstuffs, a pair of huge canvas water containers and a crate of imported Scottish whisky, packed everything on a train of three mules, saddled up one of the thoroughbred horses Lydia and he had been raising on a ranch to the south of San Francisco, and set out alone for the hills.

Himself and hundred upon hundred of others.

Gerald skirted north of Gold Run and Dutch Flat on the Bear river and headed through Rough and Ready, where his mules cost him two dollars at the toll house and his horse a quarter. He made slow, careful progress up along the Pleasant Valley road and across the South Yuba river, stopping and doing as much prospecting as he considered each site deserved. Every night, just when the fire was fading and the whisky felt good in his stomach and on the back of his throat, he wrote to Lydia and mailed the letters in batches whenever he arrived at the next settlement. Some arrived, while others didn't, and she read them with a certain cursory interest before fastening them with black ribbon and placing them in an otherwise empty drawer.

After two months away from home, his whisky all but gone and his hands and feet raw to the point of bleeding, Gerald smashed his pick against a shelf of rock in sublime anger and found himself staring at a line of solid gold more than three inches thick.

He was off in the wooded hills below Feather Falls and he rode his sagging horse through the night in order to file his claim. When he arrived home a month later, the mine was being worked eighteen hours a day by three hired Chinamen and guarded twenty-four hours a day by a Cree Indian with a head like a bull moose and a tall Norwegian who had jumped ship in order to search for gold. Lydia met him with open arms, a magnum of best French champagne and a gown of smoke-grey silk.

They had their house built in the Sierra foothills way above Spanish Flat. Lydia wanted it close enough to the snow line to feel the beauty of its coldness, stare at the way it covered everything in its path; close enough but not so close that they would be threatened themselves.

As soon as the house was finished Gerald set out for the mine on one of his usual visits of inspection and arrived to catch the Norwegian and two of the Chinese appropriating a large quantity of gold for themselves. He came at them with the Webley revolver he was in the habit of keeping in his coat pocket. The Norwegian panicked and slammed the edge of a long-handled shovel into his head, lifting away several inches of scalp and removing one eye from its socket with uncanny precision. The two Chinamen took it in turns to drive a knife in and out of his fallen body.

Lydia paid excessively to have her husband's body freighted back down to the house and buried close to the roots of his favourite Black Oak. Less than two weeks later the Chinese fell into a bitter quarrel in an opium house and killed each other. The Norwegian gambled away half of what he had stolen, drank and whored away most of the rest. When what remained was stolen from him in a drunken stupor on the waterfront, he signed on for a ship bound for Cuba. Passing Tierra del Fuego in a fierce storm he was swept overboard and presumed drowned.

By the time that happened Lydia had fallen in love for the first time. Like many women to whom this happens relatively late in life, she was all but irresistible in her passion. Jordan MacPhail married her more or less under threat. Fortunately. Lydia had sufficient of a sixth sense to ensure that there was no way he could get his hands on most of her money.

He gave her a son, whom she named Robert and doted on, even while Jordan was becoming more and more grudging with his attentions and more and more demanding in his requests for spending-money that would see him through his increasingly frequent trips to San Francisco.

Lydia gave him as little as she could to keep him quiet, loved her son all the more and despised the father to the same degree. After he returned sick with what she assumed (yet had no way of telling for sure) was a venereal disease, she hired a detective from the Didion Agency in Sacramento to follow him. When she read the report he was already too low in her regard even to be shocked; all that it did was to confirm what she had suspected. The only thing for which she could not forgive him was dragging her son's name through the smirch and stink of the gutter.

One night she plied him with brandy and champagne and

made him think she was inviting him into her bed for the first time in a long while. Naked, he cowered beneath her eyes when she showed him the detective's report of his activities. She told him that she was making him a regular allowance on condition he left the house in the morning, changed his name and promised never to attempt to get in touch with either her son or herself again.

She had ceased to think of Robert as Jordan's son also.

There was little Jordan could do but agree.

From that minute Lydia considered herself a free woman and at breakfast the following morning she told Robert that his father had died in a shooting accident in San Francisco. A fight had broken out in the street and he had been hit by a stray bullet. It had entered his brain and he had died instantly, without pain.

Robert was then a month short of his third birthday.

Lydia was no more than thirty-four but she decided that she had done with men for all time. She put a good manager into the mine, paying him the highest wages of all to secure his best service and loyalty. She took advice about investment and diversified sufficiently to treble her income over the next decade. She was a very rich, large woman who lived in a large, rich house with two servants and a cook and a handyman and – since seven weeks earlier – without her son.

That was the reason for her contacting the Didions for the second time in her life; the reason for R. G. Fowler's sweating, finally dangerous journey up through the spreading foothills and onto Bear Creek road in search of the MacPhail house. It was not quite grand enough to be called the MacPhail mansion, though some did, shaking their heads in a mixture of envy and admiration that one person should own so much.

And a woman at that.

But, 'See,' they said, 'she's lost her husband and now her son's run out on her. They ain't happy, not for all their gold.'

And they shook their heads, feeling some sorrow and not a little pleasure.

When Fowler clambered, wet with sweat and masked in trail dirt, from the chestnut's saddle, his suit was a torn rag, his dark hair tousled and unkempt, his temper that of a bear who'd been caught with his leg in a rusty trap.

He shambled a few paces towards the porch and an astonished Lydia MacPhail, her hand resting with an attempt at elegance against one of the white-painted wooden pillars.

'If you don't get back on that animal and ride out of here this instant, I'll order my men to run you out!

'Yeah,' said Fowler with a slow nod of the head. 'Yeah, that's fine. Fine.' His voice was slow and low, near enough inaudible. He made a couple of scratching gestures across his chest and said: 'Lady, I could use a drink.'

'Didn't you hear what I . . .'

'Sure I heard you. You were real good. Now about this drink . . .'

Her hand came off the pillar in the shape of a not-so-small fist. 'There is no drink!'

Fowler's nose twitched disappointedly. 'No drink, huh? Damn big place like this an' you ain't got a drink in it.' He heaved his chest forward and lumbered a few vague paces towards the porch. Lydia was certain by now that the intruder was either suffering from sunstroke or merely insane. She called aloud for the handyman, set herself across the front of the porch with her arms folded and waited for the stranger to be thrown out.

'Lady, it's hot an' I been in the saddle of that nag for a long time gettin' up here. If you've changed your mind that's okay by me, I guess, though you might've sent a wire and saved me the trouble. But if you can get one of your boys to feed an' water my horse and get me a couple of shots of bourbon, I'll be on my way.'

The hired help appeared round the corner of the house, a pick handle tapping against the palm of his open hand.

Lydia MacPhail said, 'I don't know what you're talking about.'

Fowler's shoulders lifted and fell. 'Suit yourself. Just keep that boy there away with that stick.'

'Cord, throw him out.'

Fowler gave another bear-like shrug and shifted his weight on his short legs and waited. The feller with the pick handle was maybe twenty and an inch or so over six foot. Muscles bloomed under the thin cotton of his work shirt. His eyes were bright and blue and dismissive as he waved the handle in Fowler's direction and told him to mount up and get the hell out. Fowler gave his head a shake and waited, standing his ground.

The youngster came for him then, throwing the pick handle high over his shoulder and then bringing it down through a wide curve that was aimed at the side of Fowler's skull.

But Fowler was hot and tired and sick of playing games. What's more he was thirsty. He didn't believe what the woman had said about the house being dry. One moment the length of wood was on its way down and the next it was looping harmlessly away over the grass. Cord's right arm was up tight between his shoulder blades and he was on his knees, face contorted in a scream.

The bright, blue eyes found Lydia MacPhail imploringly.

She advanced a step from the porch. 'Let him go. Let him go!'

Cord went spinning forward, arms and legs flailing. He scrambled to his feet and stood there, breathless and hurt, hugging his arm like a busted wing.

Fowler looked at Mrs MacPhail and said: 'Next time be more careful about sending a boy where only a man will do.'

Cord's eyes smarted but he held both his tongue and his ground.

Fowler scuffled his right foot and said, 'Aw, hell! The agency'll send you a bill for my time.

He was gripping the bridle when Lydia MacPhail stepped

towards him. 'You're from the agency? The detective agency?'

'I sure as hell ain't Western Union.'

'You didn't look like a detective.'

Fowler shrugged. 'It's something to do with the way I dress.'

'The last detective . . .'

'I know. Looked like Kit Carson in a three-piece suit.'

'I thought I might get the same man.'

'What I heard, you prefer to change 'em every once in a while.'

Lydia MacPhail flushed and started to say something but Fowler raised a hand apologetically and stopped her. 'Okay, I'm sorry. I didn't mean no offence an' I don't want to have to bust that kid's arm on account of you setting him on me again. Like I said, I'll report back that you got your business done some other way an' the Old Man'll send you a bill.'

'My business,' she said to his back, 'it isn't dealt with. Not at all.'

'I understood you to say . . .'

'I was confused.'

'About the drink too?'

'I'm sorry.'

'Don't be. Just level with me.'

'About my business?'

'About my drink.'

She rubbed her hands together for a moment and sighed. 'You're a very determined man, aren't you, mister . . .'

'Fowler. And about some things, yes.'

'Like your work?'

'Sometimes.'

'And alcohol.'

'Always. Now do you have any bourbon?'

She shook her head. 'I don't think so. My last husband, he may have left some behind . . .'

'He must've run out in a hurry. You set your boy on him?'

Lydia MacPhail came close to a scowl. 'For a detective you aren't very close with your tongue, mister . . .'

'I told you, Fowler. And maybe you noticed, I'm not very tall either.'

She raised an eyebrow. 'Just your thirst. All right, mister Fowler, why don't you come inside?'

As she turned and walked towards the panelled front door, Fowler noticed, a little to the right of the sullen handyman's head, a bronze statue of a hunting dog poised in the bushes, its nose pointing expectantly skyward.

Five

Cantrell's ranch was at the northern end of the Lost Creek valley, its buildings one above the other so that from a distance they seemed to be standing almost roof to floor. Closer to, it was possible to see that the land lay in broad ledges and Cantrell – or whoever had built the place – had made good use of the natural gradations. The main building was at the centre, bunkhouse and barns set above and below. Out front was a narrow corral with a high fence, some dozen or more horses bunched towards the furthest end. Cattle grazed lazily across the pasture. There were fruit trees running at an angle between the ranch house and the western slope of the valley and what looked like a large vegetable patch had been dug by the corral.

Hart and Sheriff Mosley reined in their mounts in the shelter of a bunch of juniper, most of them pushing their spread branches up some twenty feet.

Mosley switched a wad of tobacco across his mouth and

pulled a pair of field glasses from his saddle bags. He trained them on the ranch, fidgeting with the focus and cursing softly under his breath. Apart from a honey-coloured hound dog and a woman who was sitting close to the door of the main house slicing onions, he couldn't see a damn thing.

'Here!'

Hart took the glasses and made a sweep across the valley end.

'Reckon they're out checkin' stock?'

Hart handed back the glasses, shrugged. 'Could be mendin' fences, any fool thing. Then again, they could be right back of that log wall doin' nothin'.'

'What the hell'd they be doin' restin' in the middle of the day when there's work to be done?'

'Search me, sheriff. But either way, we won't find out sittin' on our asses.'

Mosley grinned and spat tobacco juice in a dark stream. 'Sounds to have a grain of truth in it. You want me to ride on ahead?'

'An' claim all the reward?'

'Now what makes you think I'd do a thing like that? Invited you along, didn't I? 'Sides, might make more sense for me to go in first. This feller Bennett proves to be who he could be, he's liable to start shootin' off every damn gun in sight soon as he sees who you are. Ain't likely to forget you, I reckon.'

Hart leaned an elbow down onto the pommel of his saddle and gazed along the valley. 'Makes sense, sheriff, only you just might be in for a little trouble.'

'How come?'

'You go in there on your own and start askin' questions and then he starts takin' target practice, it's goin' to take me some minutes to ride in an' lend a hand. Just could be too late.'

Herb Mosley leaned back his head and squinted up at the sky. 'Course,' he said after a few moments' thought, 'if I weren't plagued with this leg, that's a risk I'd take. But seein' as that's the case – and as long as you understand that – I reckon what you say's got some sense to it.'

'So we'll ride in together.'

Mosley shifted his plug of tobacco with his tongue and managed the beginnings of a laugh. 'Together,' he said.

At first they wondered if she couldn't hear them, was maybe deaf. But some slight faltering with the paring knife, a sense of rigidity which suggested a body held under tight control, told them that she knew only too well of their slow approach.

The sheriff halted his mount ten yards from the bunk house, the woman seated above him on the first ledge of land, the empty unglazed windows of the house behind her.

Hart came to a standstill a couple of yards back from the lawman and over to his right, giving his gunhand clearance and room. When Mosley talked, Hart scanned the three levels for the least sign of movement.

At first there was none.

'Your man ain't home then?' Mosley asked a second time.

'Like I said, sheriff.' Her voice was strained and worn like her face and hands, a young enough woman worn down like so many by the land. She made no attempt to keep her distaste for Mosley out of her voice and he felt no less for her on account of that.

'Any notion when he'll be back, Mrs Cantrell, ma'am?' Her feelings towards him made Mosley excessively polite.

'Some time after sundown'd be usual.' She peeled the vegetables as she talked, hardly bothering to look at either man. Dirt tracked across her hands in broken lines.

Mosley glanced round at Hart, uncertain whether to believe her and ride off or make a search of the buildings. Hart was undecided also, knowing only that the woman would try to stop them if they attempted to go past her. Of course, they had the power to force her, only . . .

'He take on any new hands lately, Mrs Cantrell?'

She did look at him then; looked at him and lied as calmly as she sliced an onion and pushed out the rounds, one after the other into the big iron pot at her feet. 'Not a one, sheriff. Can't afford more'n the one. That's Cal an' he's been with us five, no, six year.'

Mosley nodded, glanced at Hart quickly. If she was lying about that then she likely was about everything. Hart caught the sheriff's sense, felt the tension rise in the older man's body. His faded blue eyes skimmed the buildings once again and saw nothing that hadn't been there before. Off to the side the hound dog stretched and sniffed suspiciously before falling back to his lazy dream.

'I guess we'll wait, ma'am,' said Mosley and swung his leg, stiff as a poker, over the saddle.

'I told you, sheriff,' she began, but the confidence wavered in her thin voice at last as if she realized he no longer believed her.

Before Mosley got his good leg to the ground Cantrell stepped out from the house. He was wearing a white shirt loose over his work pants, like a man who might have been sleeping and just woke. A man who'd had time enough to strap his gun belt on tight.

Hart's thumb flicked the safety thong from round the hammer of his Colt.

'What's goin' on, sheriff?' Cantrell asked. His eyes shifted across to where Hart was still astride the grey, but if he recognized him, he gave no sign.

'Lookin' for a feller figured might be workin' for you. Name of Bennett.'

Cantrell shook his head and looked relieved. 'Made a trip out here for nothin', sheriff. Ain't got but one man an' he's . . .'

'Called Cal and been with you five year,' Mosley interrupted, his voice tightening with anger. 'Your wife said. I was thinkin' about a feller goes by the name of Bennett.'

Cantrell shook his head. 'I don't know no Bennett. Sure don't work for me. But if you want to stick around till Cal comes back in off the south end, you can make sure.'

Hart shifted the grey sideways to give himself a little more room. 'When we met up on the ridge a few days back, he was ridin' with you. Maybe you can't remember that?'

Cantrell looked puzzled. 'Bennett? That was his name? He never said as I recall. Went his own way not more'n a couple of miles after we quit your camp. Sure ain't round here.' He continued to look surprised. 'Bennett, I didn't know him for a Bennett.'

Mosley pulled a folded flier from his vest pocket and shook it out. 'Could be you know him as Barlow. Henry George Barlow. Killed a feller over Ely way.'

Hart imagined a movement up at the barn and his body tingled alert.

Cantrell moved back a step closer to the doorway. 'What's your jurisdiction here, sheriff?'

Somebody darted across the high arched doorway of the barn, far enough back to be no more than a scuttling shape. Hart's hand settled on the pearl grip of his gun.

'Here's my damned jurisdiction!' called Mosley and made a play for his pistol.

Cantrell surprised them all by clearing leather faster than any rancher should have been able. Mosley stood gaping as the report sang out and something hard and hot as all hell hammered through his side.

'Jesus Christ!' he called as his pistol slipped through his fingers and back down into the holster. He swayed off to the left and the support he should have had from his stick wasn't there.

As he was falling to the ground, Hart turned the grey fast and headed towards him, bending low and snapping off a couple of quick shots as he went. The first slivered several inches from the side of the barn door and the second found the empty space between Cantrell's head and the planking about it.

'Never mind me!' yelled Mosley and pushed himself up onto his knees, trying all the while to prise his gun from its holster. Both Cantrell and whoever was in the barn were firing at will and the dirt spat up wildly around the grey's hoofs.

'I said don't mind me!'

'I heard you.' Hart reached his left hand low past the saddle, seeking Mosley's own hand. The sheriff clasped his fingers tight round Hart's wrist and made as good a jump for the back of the mare as he could. He rammed his chest against the animal's withers and a second bullet went clean through his right buttock, removing a slice of flesh and leaving a channel four inches long. He yelled in anger more than pain and grabbed at the saddle and pulled hard. Hart kicked Clay with his spurs and urged her into a gallop.

When he was fifty or more yards down the valley and passing the end of the corral, he angled the grey steeply round and ordered Mosley to jump clear.

'Like hell . . . !'

'Do it!'

Mosley landed in a sprawling heap and rolled over several times, ending up with one arm twisted behind his back and the other uncertain which of his wounds to cover.

Hart rode with his body hanging low from the saddle, almost hidden from sight by the grey's head and side. One slug fell short enough to send a cloud of dirt stinging into his face, but other than that they were saving their ammunition for when they had a better target. Hart tightened his grip on the reins, shouted loud in Clay's ear and galloped her up the steep rise of ground that ran close alongside the bunk house. He lifted himself in the saddle at the last moment, hauling her into a jump almost physically. The grey's hoofs skittered the loose dirt on the ledge in front of the ranch house and held. Cantrell jutted his arm through the window to the left of the door and sent two shots directly over the saddle but Hart was no longer there.

He dived through the open doorway, tucking his head low and rolling towards the open fireplace against the back wall. He came out of it smoothly and as he righted himself the hammer clicked back on his Colt and Cantrell was crouched in front of him less than ten feet away.

'Bastard!' Cantrell hissed and threw the empty pistol at Hart's head.

He swung his head aside at the last moment and closed on the rancher fast enough to evade the arm Cantrell threw up to parry his swing. The side of the gun barrel lashed against Cantrell's temple and the sight tore a line from the eye corner to the lobe of his ear, pulling a section of the lobe away. Cantrell's feet slid from under him and Hart caught him another blow when he was on the way down, this time with the butt end hard against the base of his skull.

Hart heard the bone splinter and felt it give way beneath his hand.

Mosley's warning shout moved him fast towards the window and a bullet – from the sheriff or from Barlow he didn't know – ricocheted around the back of the room, ripping wood as it went.

Hart vaulted over the sill and as he landed in a low crouch the man he'd known as Bennett was holding a gun on him and saying: 'I should've killed you when I had the chance!'

Hart threw himself forward, head down, firing as he went. Simultaneously a pistol shot rang out from below. Barlow was slammed against the front of the ranch house, one slug embedded against the wall of his stomach, the other, taking away the front of his head above the eye line, killing him instantly.

Hart pushed himself to his feet and something shook and whirled close behind him. He turned fast with an outwards swing of the arm that sailed over Mrs Cantrell's head. Her face was white, skin drawn back over the bone like a corpse. The small knife was in her hand and aimed for Hart's belly. He backed off and Mosley yelled for her to hold still or he'd shoot but she was past hearing anything for real by now. She darted the knife in on Hart so quick he was only just able to catch her wrist in one hand and slam it down against his other arm. Her fingers flew open and the knife fell away even as her arm broke.

She spat in his face and cursed him terrible names till Mosley came up behind her and slapped her across the back of her head with his pistol cushioned inside the crown of his stetson.

They looked at the lifeless outlaw sprawled bloodily against the wall.

'That him?'

'Guess so. Looked pretty like that picture till his face got changed some.'

'Reckon they'll still pay up on the reward?'

'They'd better.'

'Yeah. How 'bout the other feller?'

Hart jerked his head towards the door.

'Dead?'

'Uh-uh. Just out cold.'

Mosley wandered over and took a look. 'How come he opened up like that?'

Hart shrugged. 'Remember what it said on that flier. "Three others unknown". Likely he was one of them.'

'Yeah. Could be.' Mosley was looking pale and having difficulty standing up, even with one hand resting against the wall.

'What we goin' to do about her?' asked Hart, nodding towards Mrs Cantrell.

'Wait till she comes round. Take her in with Cantrell if she wants. Otherwise leave her here. That's okay with you? It was you she was tryin' to gut with that knife of hers.'

Hart nodded. 'Fine by me. Now what say we get them wounds of yours staunched before you lose so much blood you faint away.'

Mosley looked indignant. 'Hell, boy! Man like me ain't goin' to pass out over a couple of little scratches like that! Huh!' He laughed and Hart was only just quick enough to catch him when he fell.

*

They rode back towards Virginia City with Barlow's body wrapped in a sheet of tarpaulin and draped across a mule from the ranch stock. Cantrell and his wife rode with their hands tied in front of them, the ropes secured to the pommels of their saddles, and from there to the sheriff's own mount. Cantrell was also tied at the legs, the rope fastened under the horse's belly. Hart and Mosley took it in turns to stand guard the nights they were on the trail. When they got back to Virginia City a crowd got together on the street and watched and cheered and jeered and all Mosley wanted to do was get his ass off the back of his animal and onto something soft.

Cantrell refused to admit having anything to do with the bank hold-up in Egan County. Claimed never to have heard of anyone called High-Hat Thomas or Cherokee Dave Speedmore. Opened fire on Mosley and Hart because he reckoned they were trespassing on his land without the proper authority. Sure he'd known that Bennett was up in the barn but figured he was keeping out of sight because Hart had come to get him after their quarrel back on the trail. Didn't have the least idea that he was also called Barlow or that he'd killed a bank manager or anyone else.

Mrs Cantrell didn't say a thing, simply sat in the cell and seethed.

Mosley sent in a claim for the reward on Barlow to the head office of the Nevada Mining Company and wrote to the sheriff of Egan County, asking if there was anything that would tie in a rancher by the name of Cantrell with the Ely robbery. He knew if nothing came of it, there wouldn't be anything else to do but let the Cantrells go, maybe slap a fine on them for assaulting a peace officer in the course of his duty but even that could be chancy if Cantrell opted to complain to the circuit judge or the US marshal about his crossing the county line with no more than a nudge and a wink from the local lawman.

All this took a couple of days and it wasn't until the end of it that a hefty man with an eye-shade and a twitch in one eye stopped Hart in the street and asked him if he had a first name of Wes and if he was expecting any mail. The first letter was in a long brown envelope and had been forwarded five times, chasing Hart clear across two states. It was a reply from a cattle association high on the Missouri, informing him that they were sorry but were turning down the offer of his services as a regulator in favour of a man named Artie Penn. The letter had been mailed close on a year ago.

The second envelope had only been forwarded twice. It didn't weigh more than pigeon feathers and the writing on the envelope was purposefully buckled and curled, ends of the *n*'s and *r*'s stretching down. Hart held the envelope fast as if it might stop his breath: the calloused whorl of his thumb slid heavily across the writing. He turned away from the man at the counter and stared out into the street and for maybe ten seconds he couldn't see anything other than a sharp haze of dust.

Then he pushed the envelope, unopened, down into his rear pants pocket and strode out. He walked past Mosley's deputy on the street without a sign of recognition though by now he was seeing things clearly enough. He went into the cantina at the edge of town and bought two bottles of tequila. He took them over to a table that he wedged into the back corner and sat down with his hat pushed back on his head and his pistol right there on the table by his hand.

Half-way down the second bottle he fell asleep in the same position, shoulders and head slumping forward a little but nothing more. The owner of the cantina hovered for a while as close as he dared and then went running for the sheriff. Mosley came hobbling painfully down, taking more weight on his walnut stick than he'd been used to. One look at Hart and he told the owner to let him sleep it off and hobbled back to his office, sending the deputy down to stand guard until Hart was able to look after his own hide again.

By the time Hart eventually came round it was well past midnight and the only other people left in the cantina were its owner and the deputy, playing cards. He groaned some from the pain in his temples and the crawling feeling in his gut and hated his mouth for tasting like two weeks in the desert. It took him fully a minute to remember the unread letter in his back pocket and then he unstoppered the second bottle of tequila and drank it steadily, determinedly down.

Before dawn was really up, he set off for the livery and got his horse saddled up and pushed the folded envelope deep into one of his bags. He ate a breakfast near twice his normal appetite and swallowed down four or five cups of strong black coffee before Mosley hobbled in and told him two wires had come – one from Egan County saying they knew nothing on which to hold Cantrell, the other addressed to Hart from a man by the name of Fowler at the Didion Detective Agency.

Six

Hart reined in the grey hard as a cyclist swerved out from Geary onto Market, peaked cap pulled low across his eyes, iron-spoked wheels whirring to a blur. The mare tossed her head and her mane shimmered momentarily in the sun as it reflected sharply from the glass windows. A tall woman, her blue check dress bustling out behind her, paused and turned her head. Hart caught her eye as he used his hand to calm the grey down. The woman's face nipped into a frown and she swished on her way.

The planking was being renewed on the opposite side of the boardwalk, some seventy-five yards of it. Chinese and Irish labourers worked in gangs, tools leaning against the fronts of buildings and ragged-looking horses standing patiently between the shafts of squat wooden carts filled with sand and stone and dirt.

The Palace Hotel stood seven storeys tall and filled an entire block stretching back from a frontage on Market Street that was close to three hundred feet wide. The store windows were filled with expensive and fashionable goods and between them curved steps led down from the gilt and glass front doors. A white-haired commissionaire waved Hart unceremoniously round onto New Montgomery Street and the side entrance.

Inside he found himself in a warren of carpeted floors with marble surrounds, marble pillars and pink walls. The main hotel office was flanked by a variety of other partitioned rooms: a book and magazine store, a telegraph and postal office, at least two dining rooms, a barber shop, a billiard room with a dozen tables, committee rooms, a travel agent's, a music room, a reading room, the inside display windows of the stores that faced out onto the street, and a luxuriously appointed bar complete with white marble vases holding deep green plants, a patterned carpet into which a man's boot heel was in danger of sinking without trace and, sitting alone within easy reach of the door, the bear-like figure of R. G. Fowler.

The two men shook hands and the detective growled a greeting while a uniformed waiter hovered to inquire what Hart intended to drink. Fowler intercepted with an abrupt order for another large bourbon and ice and for Hart a malt whisky imported from Scotland.

Fowler's suit had been cleaned and mended and was sufficiently presentable to make Hart feel a trace conspicuous in his trail clothes. Nobody else seemed bothered and the smooth warmth of the whisky helped Hart to feel more at ease.

'Some place!' he said finally, sitting back and staring up at the high, decorated ceiling.

'Hate it!'

'Then how come. . . ?'

'I hate it 'cause it's full of cheap gamblers and expensive whores and folk who never did a day's work in their lives! Asked you to meet me here because they serve good bourbon and I wanted you to taste that malt you got there. Also figured you deserved one good meal before you make up your mind about the proposition.'

Hart leaned forward again. 'Which proposition's that?'

'The one I'm goin' to make when you got some good food inside you.'

He obviously wasn't going to reveal more until then. The pair lapsed into desultory conversation which served to fill in some of the time that had passed since Fowler had ridden off from where Hart left him, taking along with him that spunky little Alice Kennedy, all eyes and buck teeth and guts.

When they moved along to the dining room with its solid silver cutlery and Irish linen tablecloths the meal proved to be every bit as good as Fowler had promised.

The detective ordered for both of them. Oxtail soup followed by baked trout, a pause for a couple of drinks since Fowler refused to be bothered with wine, then haunch of venison in port wine sauce with sweet potatoes, cabbage and squash. Fowler made Hart have a rum omelette while he simply watched and drank more bourbon. They carved some generous slices of cheese, after which Fowler broke his drinking habit long enough to open a bottle of brandy and light two long Cuban cigars.

'It's a missing kid job,' he said, dropping the match into an oval silver ashtray.

'Girl?'

Fowler gave a short shake of the head. 'Boy.'

'How old?'

'Sixteen.'

'Then he ain't lost.'

'No?'

'Not at sixteen. He's missin' cause he wants to be.'

A shrug of heavy shoulders followed by a cloud of upward-drifting smoke. 'Does that matter?'

'Makes him a sight more difficult to find for one thing.'

'And the other?'

'When he is found he likely won't want to come back.'

Fowler rolled the brandy round the balloon glass and gulped some down. His smile came slowly and only lived around the eyes. 'One more reason why I don't want to do this thing alone.'

'Go on.'

'You know how many kids go missing every year in San Francisco, Wes? Hell, every damned month. Every week. There's sections of this city it ain't safe for most folk to go into without eyes in their asses an' pockets weighed down with guns.'

Hart nodded with some little surprise, though believing what the detective said. 'How come you're not using another man from the agency?'

'For one thing they got more pantywaists than anything else. For another the Old Man's got 'em prancin' around all over the state. He gave me fifty dollars flat rate to hire someone to help out.'

'Fifty dollars!'

'Well, I got this arrangement with Mrs MacPhail, she's the one whose son took off. I levelled with her an' told her we was understaffed and anyway findin' some youngster who'd headed out for San Francisco wasn't too likely. She agreed this little bonus.'

Fowler's eyes twinkled in his round face.

'How little?'

'Boy, she's got more gold than any half a dozen other folk you can name. We find him we're set up for . . . well, for a month or so.'

'An' if we don't?'

One of Fowler's stubby hands hit the table hard enough to make the knives and forks sound like an untuned carillon and bring two waiters forward in a sedate version of a run. 'Goddam! I'd managed to forget what a miserable son-of-a-bitch you are!'

Hart grinned and shook his head and tipped an inch of ash from the end of his cigar. His stomach felt full enough to keep him content for a week; the brandy lacked the smoothness of the malt whisky but made up for it in strength. He hadn't imagined feeling so good inside a place as off-putting as the Palace Hotel.

'What d'you say?' Fowler asked.

'Came all this way, didn't I?'

'You could go back again.'

'I got nothin' to go back for.' He'd managed not to think about the letter for long enough to have almost convinced himself it had never caught up with him. The knowledge that it was still there in his saddle bag waiting to be read sent a quick jolt of pain across his eyes.

Fowler saw it and noted it but said nothing and asked no questions.

'How does she know he came here?' Hart asked, shifting his position on the padded chair.

'Someone saw him. Up by Yerba Buena. With a girl. Part-Indian.'

'How long since?'

'Couple of weeks.'

Hart drank a little more of the brandy and tried to pretend he was thinking about finding a sixteen-year-old-boy. Fowler shoved the stopper down into the top of the bottle and said they'd take it with them and watch some billiards, maybe try a game or two. He called for the bill and didn't blink as he laid down thirty-five dollars in the manner of a man who did such things every other day of the week.

Fowler persuaded Hart to try his hand at the tables and succeeded in winning back most of the money he'd spent, his skill with the cue belying the amount of alcohol he'd consumed.

'Got a room?'

'Uh-uh.'

'We can double up.'

'Here?' asked Hart incredulously.

Fowler grinned. 'The good widow MacPhail ain't puttin' up this kind of money. No, we'll be stayin' at the Union up on Kearney. They ain't got the same class of bugs as this place, but the sheets are cleaned and darned and they stable mounts better'n most places in town. Okay?'

'Sure. We leavin' now?'

Fowler's grin spread clear across his face. 'Just one more game. Same stakes.'

Seven

Wes Hart woke sticky with sweat that lay on his body like cloying vomit, turning cold. He didn't know what his dreams had been, forgot them in the act of waking; he could have guessed but instead threw back the sheet and washed himself down in water from the enamel jug on the wash stand by the window. Below, the street was taking shape through a rising mist that had come in off the bay during the night. Light, yellow and sickly, began to filter through the narrow angles between buildings.

Two rooms along, Fowler clutched his pillow in sleep. For him it was the same old dream, the Giants were into their final innings and they were a score down. Fowler was strutting out towards the mark, bat gripped tight between confident hands, the crowd on its feet and cheering him on each step of the way. He licked his teeth with the end of his tongue, shifted the angle of his peaked cap and dropped into a cocky little crouch, head angled round towards the pitcher's mound. For long seconds it seemed as if the ball would never leave the man's hand, then there it was swinging in a wicked curve towards him. Fowler's tongue pressed hard against the roof of his mouth and he began his strike . . .

The thud of the pillow against the side wall awoke him in time to hear the shout of protest from the adjoining room; in time to see the same pillow rebound against the tall jug and send it down against a china bowl, pitching its contents forward to the floor.

Fowler cursed in a growling complaint that brought its echo from next door.

'Shit!' The detective's hands pressed against his temples as the pressure of his feet on the thin carpet sent waves of discomfort jarring through his head.

He stumbled as far as the wall and hammered with the side of his fist, increasing his own head pains but shutting up his now frightened neighbour. Fowler splashed water in the general direction of his face and avoided looking at the fur on his tongue in the smeared and chipped mirror that hung from a loose nail in the wall.

He had a theory that if a man could drink enough and pass through all the horror and obscenity of hangovers and throwing up on his hands and knees in the nearest back alley, then he should reach a state of perfection in which all distress and pain was left far behind. He hadn't achieved it yet but a lack of success wasn't going to stop him from carrying on with his efforts.

For now, though, his head felt like it had been kicked at hourly intervals by a relay of mules and his mouth had the taste of something scooped up from where they were dredging the bay.

He pulled on a miscellany of clothes and joined Hart below, drinking his breakfast and doing his best not to look at the ham and eggs and grits that Hart was forking into his mouth – to say nothing of the short stack of pancakes with maple syrup and butter. Fowler even grimaced at a harmless cup of coffee. He hung in though and by the time Hart had satisfied his morning appetite, he was ready to tell him what he knew about Lydia MacPhail's missing son and his supposed girl friend.

Robert MacPhail was five-nine, having sprung up three inches since his fifteenth birthday. He was lean to the point of being called skinny, his arms gawky and forever giving the impression of being too long for his body. He had sandy hair that flopped across his forehead, grey-green eyes, and skin that had a tendency to take on freckles when exposed to a deal of sunshine. He'd never seemed interested in anything overmuch, just mooched around the way youngsters did, passed through phases of being keen on horses and such and maybe the only thing that had stuck was a fondness for guns and hunting. There were a lot of mornings when he'd be out before the light had really spread, taking a couple of dogs and maybe one of the hired men with him: he'd come back with anything that flew or ran on four legs. Throw in his haul at the back door for the kitchen. Usually refuse to eat it when it got to the table.

He'd inherited some of his father's wildness and unpredictability, although it had hardly ever showed through until the last year or so before he'd run off. Then there'd been sudden outbursts of temper in front of his mother; stubborn refusals to do things he'd previously accepted; an incident she'd never successfully got notions of, when he'd dragged back one of the gun dogs with great welts across its body, its coat matted with blood and mud. He'd run off three or four times, taking a gun with him and some ammunition and supplies he'd taken from the house. On each occasion when he'd returned he'd said nothing about where he'd been, how he'd coped up in the hills with only himself for company.

Lydia quizzed him each time, accepting more and more readily his silence and trying not to notice that it bordered on contempt. She thought of his trips as a kind of testing of maturity, a growing-up ritual similar to those she'd heard took place among the Indian tribes.

So far he'd always returned.

When he didn't, she'd waited and waited before sending out the men from the house to search for him. Waited longer before calling in the detective agency.

A little more than two weeks before, one of Mrs MacPhail's men had seen someone he was almost prepared to swear was Robert down near the bay at Yerba Buena Cove. He'd looked thinner than before as if food had been hard to come by; his clothes had been torn and soiled and he'd been walking fast, scurrying along as if not wanting to be seen. There'd been a girl with him, short, dark-haired, a honey sheen to her skin: a half-breed Indian, even an Apache, the man thought.

He'd called out Robert's name and all he'd got in response was a hasty glance and the scurrying had shifted up into a run, the girl keeping pace. It hadn't been the sort of area the man had felt safe exploring on his own. All he could do was pass on the information to Mrs MacPhail when he got back north of Sacramento and up into the hills.

It was the only recent information Lydia MacPhail had been able to give to Fowler and now he'd moved it along the line to Hart, who was wiping a chunk of dark bread round his plate, mopping up whatever there was to savour.

'Ain't a whole lot, is it?

'No. Not in a place this size, it ain't.'

'Think we got a chance?' Hart licked at the ends of his fingers, then sat back and belched contentedly Three or four people looked round and a woman breakfasting with her husband pulled in her waist tight and tutted.

'He's still with the girl maybe we got a chance. Gettin' folk to remember two like that's easier than one.'

'If it was him the feller saw in the first place.'

Fowler sighed. 'We just got to hope it was. Work on that, anyways. Ain't got nothin' else. He could be any damned place in the state by this time.'

'Yeah.' Hart pushed his plate away and set an arm along the table. 'Where do we start? Down by this . . .'

'Yerba Buena. Yeah, guess so.'

'We splittin' up or what?'

A gruff laugh came from Fowler's mouth and he wiped finger and thumb across his thick moustache. His eyes seemed smaller than ever in the early part of the day, the skin puffed up around them as if trying to squeeze them out or cover them over completely. 'Down on the waterfront you guard my back an' I'll look after yours an' if we're lucky we'll get back out of there with our money belts still on and without someone sneakin' a blade between our ribs.'

Hart looked a shade disbelieving.

'Tell you something, Wes. The population of this place's gone up treble in the last ten years. Some of them's folk with money, the sort that eat where we was last night. Eat there every damned night an' never think a thing about it. An' for every one of those there's ten, twenty, thirty more as come here without a dime and soon they got even less than that. They sleep in flophouses if they're lucky and if not they sleep rough. They'll get food by beggin' or stealin' or any way they can. If they're young enough and good lookin' enough, girl or boy, they'll sell themselves to the highest bidder till the disease gets 'em so they can't run that trick no more. There's gangs of kids roamin' parts of San Francisco – no more'n a couple of blocks from where we was up to our asses in silver an' marble – who'll attack anyone fool enough to walk their way. Three minutes or less an' they'll have the clothes stripped off his back, his money'll be gone and as like as not he'll have been garroted and left for dead. If Robert MacPhail's gone to ground in this city, as likely as not that's the kind of company he'll be keeping. An' I don't aim to wander into that sort of thing on my own.'

Hart set his hands to his back just above the waist, stretched backwards and yawned.

'Just so long as you're that wide awake,' said Fowler, 'we shouldn't be in for any trouble at all.'

'That's right,' agreed Hart, standing up. 'Me awake an' you cold sober, we make a fine team.'

Fowler's growled laughter faded into a question by the

door. 'That lethal little toy you was totin' round when I saw you last – you still got that?'

'You mean the sawn-off?'

'That's the one.'

'Sure. Back in my room.'

'Bring it along.'

'You want me to walk through San Francisco brandishing a shotgun? What the hell are the local law goin' to think about that?'

Fowler scratched at his gut. 'Let's get one thing clear before we start. There ain't enough police on the pay roll here to get even half-way close to cleanin' up the crime in this city. Which means that most of the time they don't even try. An' those that do are soon bought off with bribes. Not all of them, but most. Ain't no way round it. Not with stayin' alive too. On top of that the places we're goin' to be lookin' for Robert MacPhail ain't seen no policemen for so long they wouldn't recognize one if he stepped up to 'em and tapped 'em on the shoulder to wish 'em a good day.

'No, you forget about the law like they already forgot about you the minute you step out from some well-lit street and into an alley. Bring that little beauty along, right enough. You don't have to wave it in the air all the time, just make good an' sure it's to hand. Never know when we're goin' to be glad of that little extra help.'

The shotgun was a Remington ten-gauge, its twenty-eight-inch barrels sawn down to less than half their original length to give a wider blast pattern and make the weapon more manoeuvrable. Hart loosened the buckle of his gun belt one notch and slipped the Remington down into the left side of the belt, the trigger guard resting against its edge. He slung his Indian blanket over his right shoulder and knotted it loosely below his left hip, covering the shotgun at the same time as leaving his right arm free to use the Colt at his hip.

Remembering what Fowler had suggested they might come up against, Hart didn't leave things at that. From his bags he drew the double-action Starr .44 pistol which had been his since he'd taken it from a soldier fighting for the Union in the War Between the States. Hart had lost the war and most of his prejudices along with it, but hung onto the gun.

The other weapon he removed from his saddle bags was a double-bladed knife inside its Apache sheath – like the Navaho blanket a gift from his days on the frontier scouting for the army. The knife sometimes hung from the pommel of his saddle, sometimes was hidden beneath his shirt, its loop about his neck. Now he pushed it down into the outside of his right boot, the tip of the haft less than an inch below the top curve of scuffed leather.

Armed like that he felt ready to take on whatever glories the city of San Francisco had to offer.

They started in the haybunks along Vallejo Street wharf. Scores of men and a few women lay curled up in the hay or sat, straddle-legged, hawking bitter phlegm onto the dusty floor. Bottles of rotgut liquor were passed from hand to hand and little else. Fowler went in first, his crumpled and stained suit making him appear at first glance simply another bum in search of somewhere to sleep. Then when the questions began, resentment and a kind of realization set in and silence and antagonism were only eased over by Hart's presence in the light that filtered through the slats of the doorway. The Colt at his side was enough to free a few tongues and quieten down their desire to pitch Fowler out and into the bay.

One burly Irishman shook his head of dark curly hair towards Hart and told him he was asking for trouble and that if he didn't get back where he belonged, well, he'd come across just the feller to give it to him. Hart shrugged and ignored him and told Fowler to get on with his questioning. The Irishman was broad-shouldered and sure of himself. He advanced on Hart with a length of timber held in both hands and swinging up over his shoulder like a club.

Hart shook his head sadly and sighed and waited until the timber came all too slowly for his head. He neatly sidestepped, drew his Colt in a blur of speed and laid the side of the barrel against the Irishman's temple. The length of wood spun from between his hands and he struck the stone floor face first, splitting his nose open like some damaged fruit.

After that Fowler got himself a lot more attention but nothing that he heard was any use at all. Most of the men claimed not to have seen the gangling sandy-haired youngster either in the company of a breed girl or on his own. Most of them wouldn't have remembered the last face they saw before they fell asleep. After something over an hour Fowler had had enough.

The light was so bright off the bay they had to shield their eyes. Out in its midst islands heaved up darkly like the humps of whales. The curve of land at the far side showed green with trees and the wind salted their tongues with the ocean. Fowler rested a boot on one of the worn wooden bollards used for securing ropes and pulled a flask from his pocket. He took a couple of quick shots and offered it across to Hart, who shook his head, 'No, thanks.'

Fowler grunted and slipped the flask back from sight.

'Ragtown,' he said.

Ragtown was the name locals had given to the city dump that lay south of Townsend Street and close by a more southerly stretch of the bay where they'd started dredging and reclaiming the land. More than a couple of hundred lived here, using whatever others had thrown out, whatever had been pulled down or broken up to fashion makeshift homes of their own.

A haphazard jumble of shacks made from odd lengths of timber and pieces of tin sheeting seemed to fill every piece of part-way level land the dump offered. Between and before them were puddles of blackened water which stank of urine and on which human excrement floated.

Hart stood still and stared and shook his head.

'Pretty, ain't it?' Fowler took another pull on his flask and this time Hart didn't even wait to be asked. The jolt of the bourbon shook the stench from the back of his throat and nose but even as he passed back the flask he knew it was no more than temporary.

'I spent time with so-called savages,' he said sadly. 'Indians like the Navaho, even the Apache. Them savages ain't got anywhere near the squalor an' stink of this . . . this . . .'

He gestured with his hand, failing for a word.

'This civilization.' Fowler offered.

Hart cleared his throat and spat, trying not to notice where a child, pot-bellied and naked and no more than two years old, sat happily playing with whatever mess it had found in one of the pools of filthy water. Off to the side, sitting cross-legged outside a shack and biting at the knuckles on the back of her scabbed hand, a woman who might or might not have been the child's mother watched abstractedly.

'We ain't askin' questions round all these?' Hart said.

'No. These places usually throw up some sort of leader. We'll talk to him. That'll do it.'

'How d'we . . . ?'

But Hart's next question was answered by the appearance of a squat figure off to the right, a man with no hair to speak of on his head yet a full beard that was turning to white from the edges inwards. He was wearing a heavy patchwork coat, oblivious of the heat, and long sailor's boots which squelched and splashed through the mud when he walked. He was stocky and might have been strong before he started going to seed. Still, at one time he'd clearly proved himself the strongest man in Ragtown and now he marched through a welter of shit and slime to prove it.

Three men came behind him, each of them skinnier and taller and younger than he was himself. One of them had hair that was long enough to reach midway down his back and large black eyes that seem to glow brighter and brighter the nearer he got. All three were armed with makeshift clubs and the leader had an old sabre clutched in his left hand, the other hand bunched into a huge fist.

Fowler growled and spat and waited.

Folk peered out from their hovels and gazed on, a few

with excitement but most of them impassively. Whatever went down it wasn't likely to bring them anything more to eat or drink. It wasn't as if a couple of stray dogs had been fool enough to wander into the camp and offer themselves up for their cooking pots. They hadn't got down to eating human flesh yet, though some of them had been sorely tempted.

Fowler and the camp leader stood and glowered at each other for several seconds until the leader's voice rasped out: 'You ain't welcome here, mister!'

Fowler nodded and continued to eye the man with distaste, taking his time and refusing to be bullied into anything that suggested he might be afraid.

'You in charge here?' he finally asked, no attempt to disguise the scorn in his voice.

'Sure I am! What the hell's it look like!'

'Look like!' Fowler spat. 'Looks like a stinkin' pile of moose turd with a handful of scum floatin' round on top.' His finger jutted forward. 'You're in charge that makes you the biggest turd of 'em all.'

The leader stumbled a pace back in surprise at Fowler's audacity and one of his lieutenants let out a howl more of pain than of surprise. Before the man could bring up his sabre or any others could begin to wave their clubs, Fowler's hands had come up out of his coat pockets and in one of them there was a pistol, its hammer ready cocked. The other held maybe twenty dollars in bills.

The money stayed in view for ten seconds before disappearing from sight: the gun remained where it was.

'All right,' Fowler said, taking pains to talk both clearly yet quietly, so that his voice wouldn't carry far beyond the immediate group of men. 'You can have it either way you want it. Between us, we can likely leave you squirmin' in the mud with blood drainin' from your guts. Then again, you got that money comin' to you for answerin' a couple of questions and answerin' 'em straight. Now which is it goin' to be?'

The four men looked at one another, undecided. Fowler

made a few grumbling sounds to show he was getting impatient and Hart kept half an eye on the feller with staring eyes and long hair and still managed to see a kid of about twelve or thirteen creeping round the shacks towards them from the side. There was something clutched behind his back and it could have been a bunch of flowers or a note saying welcome but Hart didn't think so.

'How much money you got there?' asked the leader.

'Enough.'

'We want . . .'

'You'll take what you get supposin' you're lucky enough to get anything at all. Now make up your damned mind cause this stench is gettin' up my nose and I'm likely to throw up any minute.'

'Okay,' said the man, 'tell us what you wanna know.'

'Out here?' said Fowler. 'Where everyone can see what you're gettin' for informing?'

The camp leader gave one shrug of shoulders that were beginning to go to fat and turned around, pushing his way through the three taller men and leading everyone towards a shack over by the back boundary.

There was little to tell that it was any different from the rest, save that there was more tin than wood in the construction and the side wall was painted with the name Deke in foot-high letters.

'That you?' Fowler asked, nodding.

'Yeah,' said the man and swatted at a sallow-faced woman who could have been any age between eighteen and thirty-five, clearing her out of the way. She ducked inside and immediately was greeted by the sound of children's voices, demanding food with all the blind insistence of birds in a nest.

Fowler told him what he wanted to know and Deke listened carefully, the three who formed his private army craning their necks to hear. But when Fowler had finished, the man's face stayed blank until he'd scratched at his stubble and the spots that blotched his nose and cheeks for long enough to make something up. It was so obvious that Fowler shut him up with a shout of barely suppressed anger and told him if he wasted his time with stupid lies the money would disappear out of the camp with him and straight away.

Deke moaned and cursed but stopped bothering to lie. He admitted he hadn't seen anything of a kid who looked like Robert MacPhail hanging out with any Indian girl. Then he hunched his shoulders forwards and tried not to hear the clamour that was going on behind him, his woman trying to quieten down the kids' hunger.

Hart half-turned slowly and then made the rest of the movement fast. Three strides took him to the back of the adjoining shack and he seized tight hold of the arm of the kid who'd been following them. The kid kicked out as he was lifted off the floor, one of his feet landing low in Hart's stomach. Hart continued to shake him until a rusty blade fell from one of the kid's hands. Hart stared long enough into his face to make him look away and then dropped him heavily enough to wind him.

'Get him out!' called Deke to one of his men, and the youngster was hauled to his feet and dragged screaming across the dump.

'How 'bout the money?' Deke said, traces of self-pity showing through the bragging voice. 'I told you all I could.'

Fowler's hand was still in his pocket and the shrill shouts of the children still came from the inside of the shack. He pulled out the bills and tossed them down into the man's lap. A thick-fingered hand covered them almost before they'd landed.

'Let's get the hell out of here,' said Fowler under his breath, turning towards the entrance to the dump and gesturing for Hart to follow. 'Ain't long before they realize that ain't all I got on me an' there's about enough of 'em to get it, guns or no guns.'

They walked out through the shacks as steady as they could, refusing any temptation to hurry and paying as little attention as they could to the men and women and kids who held out their hands and begged for food or money.

Hart turned at the entrance and saw that Deke had come some yards of the way after them but no further. Fowler called him to hurry. He hesitated a moment longer, wondering why the tall man with long hair and black eyes wasn't with the rest. Then he strode after Fowler and discovered the answer. Somehow the man had cut through the shanty town and made it out onto the winding road that led up from the wharf. He stood blocking their way, his eyes darker and more alive than ever, the wind off the ocean blowing his hair out in a black halo around his head. It wasn't easy to decide if he looked more evil than insane.

Eight

He was still hanging onto the length of timber he'd been threatening to use as a club back inside the shantytown, only now it tapped against the outside of his leg harmlessly. He didn't seem to have any other weapon, nothing that was stopping Hart and Fowler from simply pushing past and carrying on their way – nothing save the expression in his eyes, the sense about him of something strange, something other.

'What you want, feller?' asked Fowler, letting it be seen that his hand was back in his pocket and wrapped around the grip of his gun.

'Talk.' The answer was fast, breathless, accompanied by a worried glance over towards the camp.

'What about?'

'Kid.'

'What kid?'

'You said. In there. Kid.' Another worried look sideways, worried and hasty.

'What kid?'

His eyes blazed. 'You said. Kid with fair hair. Girl.'

'What about him?'

The wood held fast against his leg. 'I know.'

Fowler pulled from his pocket not the pistol but a few dollar bills. The effect was almost the same. 'Tell me,' Fowler said, but he was already backing away, more frightened of Deke and his particular form of primitive retribution than anything else.

'Come,' he said over his shoulder, speaking through a flurry of dark hair. 'You follow.'

Fowler shrugged at Hart, turned quickly the other way as a shouting set up at the other side of the dump. He nodded and Hart confirmed it and they both set off after the tall man who was half-running down towards the wharf. Short of the bay he turned sharp left, almost as quickly right and then left again, wanting to be certain that if Deke was following they had lost him. Ten minutes on he leaned against the wall of a warehouse and breathed: 'Twenty dollars.'

Fowler shook his head abruptly and his hand sliced the air in a brisk cutting gesture. 'Five.'

The dark eyes dilated. Fingers scratched against the planking. 'Ten.'

'Five.'

The sickly stink of rotting tomatoes slid out from the warehouse.

'Five,' agreed the man. 'Now.'

'No. Later.'

Hart watched the eyes begin to roll and thought that the detective had pushed too hard, stood too firm. But the man pushed himself off the wall and carried on in his previous direction, now quicker than ever, causing Fowler to trot. Within a hundred yards the detective was blowing hard and the air scratched up from his lungs angrily. Hart ran on ahead and grabbed the man by his shoulder, telling him to slow back down.

He shook his head so that his hair flapped like wings.

'Lose him,' said Hart pointing back, 'you lose your five dollars.'

He slowed down. He led them into a run-down area back of Market Street, already beginning to fall down through natural decay aided by earthquake and fire. A sign, brightly painted and stuck in a mound of bare earth, proclaimed Pleasant Valley with hopeless optimism. They were on the block between Second Street and Third, a row of cheap hotels and rooming houses that made anyone who wasn't broke or desperate quicken his pace and avert his eyes.

The feller leading them slowed down.

Stopped.

His index finger pointed towards a buckled door partly covered with flaked yellow paint like it had some virulent fever. There was a pane of glass above the door that was thick with dust and dirt and cracked like a spider's web. The sign hanging alongside declared Bay Hotel but the stench of the street blocked out the smell of the ocean.

'He's here?' Fowler demanded.

The man's hand was out for his five dollars.

'Is he here?'

'Five.'

'The kid first.'

The eyes came suddenly open and Hart got ready to grab him, thinking he was about to take off down the street.

'Top floor. He was there. Man with grey hair.'

'What damned man with grey hair?'

'They were there.'

'When, for God's sake?' Fowler reached up his hands and grasped his greasy shirt.

'Upstairs. Top floor.'

'I said *when*, you shit, not where!'

He shook him some more and the feller looked down on

him curiously as if whoever was being shaken was someone only distantly connected with himself. Hart wondered if he'd been taking peyote or something else.

'Is he there?' Fowler tried again, loosening his hold, shaking his head. The effort of keeping up made him cough again and he rubbed his throat below his beard.

'Is the kid up there?' asked Hart. 'Up on the top floor?'

'You said five dollars.'

'An' you promised the kid.'

'Five dollars.'

'Aw, Jesus!' said Fowler, and stuffed the bills into the man's hand. Immediately the fingers closed round them and he bolted between Hart and Fowler and down the street, making a right at the first intersection.

Hart sighed and looked towards the hotel door. 'What d'you think?'

'I think we just got suckered out of five dollars.'

But he pushed open the door nevertheless.

The stairs lacked a banister rail, they were loose and creaked each time either man set down a boot; more than one tread in every four was missing. The doors to the left off each landing were padlocked on the outside or wedged shut with pieces of wood and tied with thin rope. When they arrived on the third floor they were almost used to the stench of cabbage and vomit, stale air, cats' piss and sweat.

A body lay against the landing wall, wrapped in a torn blanket, with a couple of fingers and a patch of brownish hair poking out. Hart leaned over it and lowered his head and heard faint breathing, the thinnest wheeze from the blanket-covered mouth.

Fowler was examining the four doors. Three were locked, the fourth was open by six inches. Fowler glanced round to make sure that Hart was covering him and then used his foot to swing it back wide enough to be able to step through.

Both men waited and nothing happened.

Fowler shrugged and Hart drew his Colt and stepped inside. The air was thick and clogged with something he couldn't immediately identify. And then he looked across at one of the three beds shoved up against the walls and he could.

Everything that could have been stripped from the body had gone. A badly stained pair of long johns and one wool sock without toes or a heel were all that remained. Scabbed blood was thick down the side of the face that showed and Hart was pretty certain that more would have coagulated underneath, sticking him to the striped mattress. His legs were thin as his arms should have been, the arms little more than faintly pigmented skin stretched across bones. From the way his mouth was open and the lips swollen and purple, somebody had been ransacking his mouth for a trace of gold in his teeth.

Old bruises clung to his chest and the insides of his legs like sores that no longer had the strength to fester.

Fowler gazed down at him for just long enough and then turned away, pulling the flask from his pocket. He took a couple of good swallows before passing it over to Hart but by then the flask was more or less empty.

'How old d'you reckon he was?' Hart asked.

Fowler didn't want to look again. ' 'Bout the right age.'

'But it ain't him?'

Fowler gave a quick shake of the head. 'Let's get out of here.'

They were leaving the room when they heard footsteps coming up the stairs. Right and left of the landing they waited, guns drawn. The man who showed at the head of the stairs and turned back fast was thin like a half-starved dog and wore a bandana knotted around his head, holding down a ravaged mess of grey hair.

'Hold it!' called Hart and took a couple of strides towards the end of the landing.

The grey-haired man stopped and slowly turned. His tongue toyed nervously with the edges of his lips. He couldn't take his eyes off the dull shine of the Colt's barrel.

'Who are you?'

'Never mind.' Hart motioned him back on to the landing and he came slowly enough, watching the gun all the while.

He saw Fowler standing close by the open door and instantly began: 'Ain't nothin' to do with me. Never even took nothin' from him. Least, not less'n you count an old shirt he was wearin'. Not much left to it and what there was all bloodied up, you know, but I guess I'll find a use for it. Sell it so's I can . . .'

He fell quiet under Fowler's bearded stare.

Hart moved in close at back of him, the Colt back in its holster.

'Where's MacPhail?'

He jerked his head a little at Fowler's gruff question, but nothing more.

'Robert MacPhail.'

'Robert . . . ?'

'Sixteen. Sandy coloured hair. Maybe freckled skin.'

'What d'you say his name was?'

'Robert MacPhail.'

The grey head shook some. 'Never knew 'bout the last part. Just Bob. Bobbie she called him.'

'She?'

'The girl.'

'Indian girl?'

Another shake of the head, surprise that the stranger in the shabby suit should know so much. 'Part Apache she said. Pretty damned proud of it, too, though what she got to be proud of bein' an Indian for I couldn't never see.'

Hart eased off the wall. 'Where are they?'

He turned and looked at him with empty eyes. 'Been gone these two, three weeks.'

'You ain't lyin'?' said Fowler.

'Me? Not me. What reason'd I have for lyin'?

Fowler gestured towards the door of the open room and the man set up his hand and shook his head vigorously. 'I said, I ain't got nothin' to do with that. Nothin'. He kicked his toe down on to the boards and his eyes blinked faster. 'You ain't the law, are you?'

'Sort of,' answered Fowler.

'Reg'lar law?'

'Regular enough.'

He lifted his head and breathed deeply through his mouth, drawing in all the smells of the building like he was used to them and they gave him some kind of nourishment.

'What you want Bob for?'

'His folks want him.'

'Never said nothin' 'bout no folks.'

'Talk much, did he?'

'Not much. Him an' the girl, they whispered together times. Never knew what about.'

'When you did hear 'em, what'd they talk about? They say anythin' 'bout what they did? When they wasn't here.'

The man thought a few moments, his mouth working silently as he did so, as if rehearsing the words. 'Bob, he was lookin' for somethin'. Never did get it clear what. Somethin', though.'

'You got no idea what?'

'Not a one.'

'And the girl. What did she talk about?'

'Never said much. 'Cept to cuss. Cussed good for a girl. Good enough for any man. Tongue like a viper.'

'That all? Just cussin'?'

'She was onto Bob time to time.'

'What about?'

'Tryin' to get him to leave Frisco. Go south. Bobbie, Bobbie, she'd say, let's cut out of here and head out down towards the border.'

'Reckon that's what they did?'

He shrugged his thin shoulders. 'Who knows? Bob, he always told her it wasn't time yet.'

'What d'he mean by that?'

'Hadn't found what he was lookin' for, that's what I always figured. Whatever that was.'

'An' that's how they spent their time? Searchin' for some damn thing you don't know 'bout?'

'When they wasn't doin' what we all got to do.'

'Like what?'

The man looked at Fowler with surprise. 'Hustle some money. Get somethin' to eat. Drink. Get through another day. What else?'

'How'd they do that?'

'What Bob done, I don't know. Stole what he couldn't find, I guess. Sure was too proud to beg.'

'And the girl?'

'She done what girls always do.'

'That what she done for you to let 'em sleep in your room?'

The man shifted sideways, avoiding the detective's eyes. He wet his lips and scratched the back of his head through the bandana. A couple of grey hairs fluttered on the still air.

'They let me watch 'em. His voice was so low that neither man heard what he said.

'Speak up,' said Fowler. 'What the hell you say?'

'I said . . . I said, they let me watch 'em.'

'Watch?' echoed Hart, uncertain.

The man's face shifted sideways. 'Yeah, you know, when they was on the mattress and, well, doin' it, they let me watch. Didn't mind. Didn't do 'em any harm now did it. Roof over their heads. I never asked 'em nothin' towards the rent. Not a dime.'

He looked first at Hart then at Fowler, as if expecting them to voice some approval for his generosity. He was wasting his time. Fowler told him to open up whichever room was his so's they could take a look. Two mattresses were close together on a bare floor and not much else.

'Sure you ain't seen 'em since you said?' asked Fowler again out on the landing.

'Honest, mister. Wish I had. Good kid, was Bob.' He nodded affirmation. 'Good damned kid.'

His eyes searched Fowler's face in expectation. Fowler shoved a couple of bills down into his hand without looking.

Then he pushed past him and went down the stairs as fast as he dared without punching them through. Hart followed close behind, as eager as the detective for what south of Market passed for fresh air. Whoever had been stretched out on the landing under the old blanket had either carried on sleeping through their questioning or simply died. Either way, there wasn't anyone around to give a damn.

'Where to now?' asked Hart as soon as they hit the street.

'Shit!' growled Fowler. 'I'm goin' to fill me my flask and empty it again before takin' a bath an' washin' off as much of this stink as soap an' hot water'll shift.'

'What then?'

'We get out on the tenderloin and foul it up all over. That's what. Less you got a better idea?'

Hart had a parcel of them but none would help find Robert MacPhail. All they had was a two-week old trail that might turn out to be a lie but it was the best they'd got. 'Not me,' he said, 'you're the detective round here. I'm just watchin' your back, remember?'

Fowler remembered. He coughed and spat and got the hell out of Pleasant Valley just as quick as he was able.

Nine

The blanket hung over the back of the bed, draped down from the slightly sagging rail. Woven in red, white and dark blue, striped with a row of stretched stars along its centre and down the edges, it had been in Hart's possession more than ten, eleven years. As he sat trying to recall exactly how many, the time slipped from him, eluding him like straw cast on water and spiralling further whenever his hand plunged towards it. All that remained were fragments, snatches: the face of He Who Runs, tight and proud as he handed Hart his own chief's wearing blanket. Dogs, lean and long-toothed, curling their legs by the fire. Women pummelling corn while the young warriors sharpened their arrowheads.

'You have made peace for my people. Peace from your heart.'

Three days later the army captain had led his troop out of the fort and He Who Runs had been hacked down by a trooper's sabre. He had crawled towards the stream and let the water draw his blood out. Still it had taken him two days to die. Days of pain in which to think about his words to Hart. Peace from your heart.

The close colours of the Indian blanket blurred and for an instant Hart felt a little of the dying chief's pain and understanding. He knew himself and maybe it was his good fortune that he did not need to take a mortal wound in order to be certain: there was no peace. Least of all peace of the heart.

He realized now that he had been concentrating on the blanket to keep from thinking about something else.

The envelope was neatly folded now and lay between his spare shirt and the bottom of the drawer. Not too close to the heart, yet close enough.

He splashed water up into his face and shook his head before wiping it on the rough cotton towel. He pulled on his boots and buckled on his gun belt, lifting up the pistol and checking its load automatically, the gun's balance perfect in his hand.

Eyes staring down at the Colt still holstered at his side; that strand of hair dark across the face.

Hart lifted the Meteor off the bed and slid it down into the opposite side of his belt. The blanket he fastened over his shoulder like before. He pushed his flat-brimmed hat down on to his head and had one last quick look around the room. He opened the door, turned the key in the lock, dropped the key down into his pocket and set off for the downstairs lobby.

Fowler was sitting in a leather armchair smoking a small cigar and cradling a glass in his hand. Hart stood watching him for a few moments, thinking how little like any kind of lawman he looked. Maybe considering where they were planning on spending the evening that was just as well.

The detective turned his head as Hart approached.

'Drink?'

'Later. Let's be goin'.'

Fowler downed the remains of his bourbon. 'Pretty anxious, ain't you?'

'Anxious enough. Let's do it.'

Fowler pushed his fingers up through the sides of his beard, levered himself out of the chair. Outside the streets were busy with people, the evening was warm and would have been more so but for the breeze lifting off the bay. It didn't take them long to cut north of Market Street on to Montgomery, moving with some urgency between dawdling sightseers, their coats constantly tugged at by the hands of filthy-faced children begging.

As Hart hesitated for a moment outside a sporting goods store, glancing at the array of hunting rifles artistically arranged among a display of stuffed game birds, he sensed a movement behind him.

'Like to come home with me?'

The voice had a slight rasp to it, an edge to the invitation which suggested an uneasy urgency. Hart stared at the woman and found it difficult to believe that she was a prostitute. Perhaps the bodice of her dress was cut a little too low and revealed too much of her breasts, possibly the rouge and lipstick on her face were applied too heavily and shone too bright, her hair had an artificiality of colour that suggested paint. But she stood there smiling at him, both hands resting on the curved handle of a parasol, a small kid bag hanging from a strap about her wrist.

'Come on, dear. Only five dollars.'

Hart moved away with a stiff shake of the head, a certainty that for some reason people were staring at him, that the woman herself was laughing at his haste.

'Three dollars, dear,' came her voice, but by now she could have been propositioning someone else.

'Thought you'd got hooked,' grinned Fowler, waiting for him at the corner of the block.

Hart said nothing. He was beginning to realize that both sides of the street were busy with whores, most of them as well dressed as the women who strolled between them with their men, and paused from time to time to pass comments on what they saw in the store window. Most of the people on the street, though, were men: men in pairs, in groups of half a dozen, louder and more strident thanks to drink and the security of a crowd, men walking more furtively on their own and eyeing the prostitutes deliberately.

'Ain't shocked, are you?'

'I'd heard what Frisco was like. Just never expected it to be so obvious, I guess.'

Fowler shook his head. 'Compared to what we're like to see before we're done, this is real discreet.'

Hart shrugged the blanket across his shoulder and felt the hardness of the shotgun stock against the inside of his left arm. His hat was angled down across his forehead and the faded blue eyes took their slight shine from the street light.

'Hey, cowboy!' called a woman softly from a shop doorway. 'Why don't you come an' ride me?'

A couple of passers-by laughed as Hart shook his head and moved away, following Fowler as he threaded his way along Montgomery and right on to Pacific. Here there were less folk walking and the buildings seemed to be hotels and rooming houses rather than shops; they were a sight smarter than those they'd visited earlier in the day, steps coming down on to the sidewalk well lit from above. Occasionally a frame family house suggested that people might actually live in that city, live ordinary decent lives amongst the hordes of visitors and hustlers and down-and-outs.

A carriage rattled past and Hart glimpsed a man's face peering out, heard his voice shouting instructions to the driver.

Piano music jangled from windows and the raucous sound of male voices carolled a bawdy ballad. Fowler stepped round a drunk asleep on the boardwalk and signalled to Hart they should cross the street. The place they were heading for was three storeys high and built from brick. A man in a uniform jacket and with a gun at his hip looked both Hart and Fowler over as they approached. He didn't take to the Colt in Hart's holster and eyed the Indian blanket with a mixture of amusement and suspicion.

Fowler, though, he seemed to recognize and greeted him with a curt nod.

The two of them stepped under the red light that glowed above the panelled door and into a circular entrance hall. A Negro girl wearing a black and white maid's uniform, its skirt short enough to show the tops of her stockings, came smiling forward and asked if they'd like to leave their hats and coats. When neither did, she led them into a small parlour directly off the hall and left them there with a giggling swish of her brief skirt.

'Hello, Fowler. I thought you'd given up on us.'

The madam was sitting back of a mahogany table, long, fingerless lace gloves pulled high up her arms, a burgundy coloured dress that was more lace and ruffles than anything else piled around her body. A cigarette smoked at the corner of her mouth, jiggling up and down when she spoke.

'Where you been these months?'

'Here and there.'

She removed the cigarette from her lips, ash falling on to the polished surface of the desk. 'Always did like to be mysterious, didn't you?' She laughed and turned her attentions to Hart, looking him up and down with what appeared to be approval.

'Got a nice one there, Fowler. Friend of yours, is he?'

'Name's Hart,' Fowler introduced him. 'Wes Hart.'

The madam pointed at Hart's blanket. 'Ain't expectin' to be cold tonight, cowboy?

Hart grinned a little and shook his head.

'We got some girls here'd warm up a man three days dead!' She laughed at her joke, the cigarette back in her mouth and shedding more ash across the desk and the lace of her gloves. If she noticed either, she didn't seem to care.

'Martha workin' tonight?' Fowler asked.

The woman looked at him with a raised eyebrow. 'You an' that Martha. What is it between you an' her, Fowler? One of these times you're goin' to walk in here and she'll have gone. You know what these girls are like. Though I'll allow, Martha's a lot more dependable than most.' She waggled a finger at the detective. 'An' not just dependable, eh, Fowler?'

'She's here, then?'

'Sure, she's here. Why don't the pair of you go through and buy a drink. The champagne's improved since you were here last.'

Fowler moved towards the parlour door. 'I'll bet you're still waterin' down the bourbon, though.'

The woman laughed and turned her attentions to the man the black maid had just brought into the room. Tall and erect, his silver hair was brushed flat to his head and he was wearing a striped dress suit that looked immaculate. The cigar in his hand was the size of a Colt gun barrel. He made an extravagant bow towards the madam and started to speak to her in a mixture of German and English, his accent clipped and brisk.

Hart followed Fowler through into the first of two main rooms where the girls and their customers sat and talked and drank champagne between trips up the winding staircase between the rooms.

He stopped a short way into the room and looked round in surprise. He'd figured to have been in some pretty fancy whorehouses in his time, but this was special. The sofas and armchairs were upholstered in leather, the carpet thick enough to absorb most of a man's boot. The ceilings were high and patterned, painted pink and blue. Large oil paintings – landscapes or tigers at bay – hung in gilt frames on the walls. Through in the second room a fourpiece band played on a small stage, at that moment a brisk polka which had one girl dancing with a stiff-backed man with a military moustache.

Fowler caught hold of Hart's sleeve and pointed towards a woman with deep red curly hair and a round face rich in make-up. She was standing at the back of a settee negligently stroking the nape of a customer's neck and chatting to another of the girls at the same time.

When she saw Fowler, she stopped both activities and hurried over to greet him. Fowler wiped the lipstick from his mouth and introduced her to Hart before the three of them found a table and chairs in the back room.

The band were playing a waltz and a couple of the girls were dancing lazily in one another's arms, each wearing a few garments of satin underclothing and nothing else.

Martha had on a green dress that was open all the way down the front to reveal a great deal of her body and not very much of any other clothing. She seemed to look at Fowler with genuine affection, rubbing her fingers along the inside of his thigh as they talked.

Fowler ordered bourbon for himself, beer for Hart and champagne for Martha – partly because she genuinely liked it, but also as each girl received a bonus for every bottle of champagne one of her customers bought.

'Did she tell you when you came in?' Martha asked.

'What?'

'The bad news.'

'What news?'

'She's raised the prices.'

'On the bourbon?'

'On me. On all of us.'

'How much now?'

'Fifteen dollars.'

Fowler almost choked into his drink; Hart whistled and shook his head.

'You don't think I'm worth it?' Martha pouted, withdrawing her hand.

'Maybe,' admitted Fowler grudgingly.

She nuzzled up to him playfully. 'One of the things I've always liked about you most is how charming you can be with a lady.'

Fowler shrugged his heavy shoulders. 'I pay you fifteen dollars and then I'm the one who has to be charming?'

'That isn't funny.'

'It wasn't meant to be.'

Martha finished one glass of champagne and poured another. She was balancing a green slipper on the end of her toes, one leg crossed over the other. Hart had stared at her legs long enough to be certain how good they were; not wanting to cut in on Fowler's obvious interests, he turned and looked over the other girls in the room and stopped when he saw one with her back to him in silver stockings and high-heeled shoes and black underthings. Long, dark hair hung low down her back and she stood with one hand to her hip, legs slightly apart.

'That's Helen,' said Martha leaning forward. 'I'll introduce you. You'll like her.' She laughed. 'We can all go upstairs together.'

'Not this time,' said Fowler and as he spoke the band came to a halt and his voice cut through the general sound so that a number of people looked round.

'Not this time,' he repeated more quietly.

'What do you mean?'

'I mean this ain't a social call.'

Martha let her hand rest on his leg, looking at him and waiting.

'I'm looking for someone.'

'I thought you'd found her.' She tried a smile but it didn't quite fit.

'A whore.'

'That's what I meant.' Hart was surprised at the steel in her voice and the mixture of anger and vulnerability in her eyes.

'A breed. Half Apache.'

Martha pulled her hand away and turned her back. 'That's what you fancy nowadays, is it?'

'This is business.'

She jumped to her feet and stood there gazing down at him. 'So is this!'

Fowler hesitated a moment before drawing his wallet from his pocket and setting it down on the table next to the champagne class. He watched Martha's face as he slid out three five-dollar bills and pushed them towards her.

She closed her eyes and shook her head; sat back down. 'I'm sorry.'

'It's okay. Take the money. You're entitled to it.'

She folded it and pushed it back underneath his wallet. 'What do you want to know?'

Fowler told her. She thought for a short while and then excused herself and walked across the room and spoke with the girl she'd called Helen. After that she slipped out of sight and left the two men to their drinks and the music. She wasn't away for more than ten minutes.

'There was a girl. No one knows her name. She asked here for a job but we've only ever had one Indian girl and she ended up cutting a man's throat because of something he tried to do to her. The police raided the place and we had to stay closed for a week. No Indians since then. She tried some of the other houses I think, without any luck. Helen says she thinks she saw her on the Coast.'

'The Coast?' said Hart.

'The Barbary Coast. Up between Broadway and the waterfront. No fifteen-dollar whores there.'

'More like fifteen cents,' said Martha and went back to toying with the inside of Fowler's thigh, only this time the painted nails seemed to be reaching higher up.

'Helen says she was in one of the cribs. Someone like her, anyway. She couldn't be sure.'

'Thanks, Martha.' He covered her hand with his own but made no attempt to move it.

'We goin' to look for her now?' asked Hart.

Fowler thought about it for a whole five seconds. 'Later,' he said, smiling with his eyes. 'I reckon we can get to that a little later.'

The street was crammed with shacks no more than six feet wide, most of them just a couple of rooms, one front and the other behind. Most of the front wall was taken up by a large window and the girls sat on chairs or stretched on three-quarter sofas and posed and gestured for the men who walked past. Most wore as little as possible and those that didn't were naked. A few were pretty and some were young, but for the most part the women were plain and worn, a few truly misshapen. One hunchback sat leering out, wetting her forefinger and rubbing it slowly and deliberately round her nipples. Behind them all you could see was a narrow bed and maybe a kerosene stove or lantern, sometimes a washstand or just an iron bucket.

Hart and Fowler took one side of the street each and then the next and the one after that. They were beckoned and cajoled and cursed as they caught glimpses of men in the back rooms with most of their clothing still intact, a strip of oilcloth thrown over the foot of the rocking bed to keep the mud on their boots from dirtying the bedspread further. Hart saw one woman, a huge Negress with a scar down one side of her face, standing carelessly beside an enamel basin, one foot resting on the side of the bed as she washed with a flannel between her thighs.

They went past the Apache's crib as many as three times before Hart finally spotted her. Short, with stocky legs and wide hips but small breasts, she was shooing one customer out as she welcomed another inside.

Breed Indians might mean trouble in the posher palaces near to the centre of town, but out here on the Barbary Coast tastes were obviously different.

Hart caught up with Fowler and they waited, discouraging more than one man from standing in line. When she'd earned another dollar they moved in fast, pushing past her protests, Hart drawing the shabby length of curtain close across the casement window.

'Not two!' Her eyes were dark with alarm and she backed towards the inner room, hands at her back. 'Not two!'

'Take it easy,' Hart said, stepping past her.

'Won't take long.' Fowler set his bulk in the doorway, blocking any attempt to escape.

The girl pulled the flimsy dress round her, suddenly conscious of her nakedness, the vulnerability of her body. 'Three dollars,' she said. 'Two men at once. Three dollars.'

Fowler shook his head.

'Three dollars. You don't want to pay that go somewhere else!'

Her nose was broad and flat while the rest of her face were those of a white woman. She flicked her gaze from one man to the other and crossed one arm beneath her breasts.

'Two dollars,' she said.

Fowler shook his head.

'Two . . .'

'More.'

'More?'

'Maybe five. Ten.'

Her eyes were wider now and a sharper fear was rising inside her. She thought of calling out, but knew no one would come to her aid. She wondered how far she'd get if she ran and knew the answer only too well. The knife was below her pillow and she could slit the tall one's throat before he could draw his gun. That still left the other, the one with the beard. She sat slowly down on the bed, allowing her left hand to slide cautiously towards the soiled pillow.

'What you want to do?'

Fowler looked back at her, waiting.

'No pain. And no animals. I won't do anything with animals. Go down the street. There's a girl does it with a mule. Go . . .'

'Where's Robert?' Hart asked quietly.

It was as if he'd shouted full in her face. She rocked back on the iron bed and gripped the mattress tight.

'Where is he?' asked Fowler from the doorway.

'Who?'

'Robert MacPhail.'

'I don't know who . . .'

'Don't lie!' Fowler came forward from the doorway and she saw what might be her only chance. Her fingers darted for the knife as she leapt to her feet. Like a wildcat she sped at Fowler, the sharp blade aimed upwards to the exposed inches of flesh below his beard. She hadn't anticipated that such a clumsy-looking man would be able to move so fast. Fowler weaved the top of his body sideways as his arm slammed upwards against her elbow. The knife drove wide of his head and he punched underneath it, his fist thumping into her ribs below the heart. All the wind went out of her as he careened back towards the bed and rolled across it, the knife thrown from her hand.

When she crawled to her knees at the far side of the bed she found that she was staring down the barrel of Hart's gun.

Fowler waited for her to regain her breath and she crouched there like a caged creature, making hissing sounds as she stared back at him with hate brimming through her.

'Okay, Wes.'

Hart uncocked the pistol and returned it to his holster. Fowler set one of his boots on the edge of the bed and gave himself a drink from the flask. He offered it to the girl and she spat back at him. Fowler put the flask slowly back into his pocket and showed her ten dollars.

'We'll find him. We found you and we'll find him. All it'll take is time. You help us the money's yours and we find him faster. If you don't . . .' He glanced round at Hart suggestively.

'You were with him for quite a time. Maybe you still are. Maybe you're doin' this . . .' Fowler looked around the room with clear distate '. . . for him.' He shrugged. 'I don't know. I just want to see him, talk to him. Nothin' more.'

The girl's breathing was returning to normal. Her fear was fading now and so was her reluctance to talk. The affection she had for the boy was strong, but so was the lure of ten dollars. And maybe more.

'Why you want Robert?'

Fowler breathed out a sigh. He knew he was there. 'His mother wants to see him.'

'He hates her.'

'It's that way sometimes with kids. He'll get over it.'

She shook her head. 'He hates her.'

'Why?'

'You don't know?'

'No.'

Her hand reached towards the money. It occurred to Fowler that he'd spent most of his time giving out cash to people but he didn't care; it was Mrs MacPhail's money and not his. He let her take five dollars and held on to the rest.

'Because of his father,' she said.

'His father's dead.'

Again she shook her head. 'No.'

'Who says?'

'Robert.'

'It gets that way with kids, too. He'll get over that as well. Maybe.'

'He's alive. Down south of here. Salinas. Somewhere there.'

Fowler sat on the bed and she backed away. 'You told him that. You told him because you knew he wanted to find his father and you wanted to get him out of Frisco. You made it up.'

'No!'

'Sure you did.'

'No, Robert, he . . .'

They were interrupted by an angry shout and a man who came crashing through the door wielding a club. He was wearing a thick blue sailor's jacket and had a woollen hat pulled down over his head. He could have been the girl's pimp or a regular customer who'd lost his patience with the length of time she was taking. His mouth opened to yell something and the club began its upward swing. Hart swivelled on his left foot and hammered the barrel of his Colt against the man's forearm. Metal crunched against bone and the shout of anger was transformed into a scream of pain. Hart seized him by the back of his coat and threw him against the side wall, making the thin shack shudder. The intruder's head jolted backwards and Hart pulled away the woollen hat before slamming the reversed butt of the pistol on to the top of his skull.

It was all over inside a minute and the Apache girl could do nothing but stare in surprise. Fowler, too, was pretty admiring.

'Know him?' Hart asked, the man in a heap on the floor.

The girl's face was wide with concern. 'He owns this place. Many places.'

'You were workin' for him?' asked Fowler.

'Sort of.'

'No more you ain't.'

He was on his feet and had hold of her arm. At first she struggled but there wasn't any point. When he came round he was likely to take his temper out on her like he'd already done a few times before. And now they'd found her, these two weren't about to let her go.

'Where we goin'?' asked Hart, looking past the edge of the tattered curtain into the street outside.

'We can't take her back to the hotel, that's for sure.'

'You don't have to take me anywhere!'

'We still got business to settle,' Fowler snapped.

'How 'bout a bar?'

Fowler shrugged. 'Sure.'

The heap on the floor groaned and shifted a little until Fowler planted a kick alongside his temple and after that he was still again.

They hustled the girl out of the crib between them and headed towards Broadway. There was a small bar that Fowler visited from time to time; fair bourbon and better-than-average steaks, a piano player who didn't play too fast and who had a fine rolling left hand. The Irish barman threw a drunk off the back table and wiped it down for them, bringing Fowler his bourbon before asking the others what they wanted. He gave the girl's appearance – her face and her scanty clothes – a couple of glances but they didn't rate more. He didn't stay in business minding other folks' affairs.

Fowler took a good pull at his drink and leaned heavily forward, asked the first question.

Ten

The way the girl told it, Robert MacPhail had gone as far undercover in San Francisco as he could. Worried that his mother would do right off what she'd finally got round to – hire someone to find him and drag him back – the kid had burrowed deep into the city's rotten underbelly and stayed hid. He'd made a living as best as anyone could. When the little money he'd been able to steal had run out, he'd resorted to the usual ways of putting food in his mouth and keeping some kind of shelter over his head. Some nights that didn't matter a damn and Robert would sleep in the open on the damp wood of the wharfs or join others in the furled sails of boats anchored in the bay. When the weather got rough and the mist came in thick off the ocean it was different and he went the round of flophouses and shanty towns along with every other drifter there was.

That was how he'd met the girl. She woke up one morning with cramp along one leg and her neck stiff from a draught and found someone's body squashed up against hers. Not in any kind of sexual thing, simply another person searching for warmth. She'd dragged her leg out from underneath his and sat rubbing life back into it; spoken to him when'd he woken up and the two of them had set off to steal bread from one of the bakeries without discussing it first. They simply did it because it seemed the thing to do.

They were together a couple of weeks and somehow ran into the man with grey hair Hart and Fowler had already run down. He offered them the use of an old mattress on the floor of his room and the girl had questioned him about how they were going to pay him for it – knowing that in their world like any other no one gives anything for nothing – guessing what his answer would be. She figured he'd want to spend time with her and if not with Robert, who was certainly good-looking enough for any man whose fancies were set that way. But taking part wasn't what he wanted.

Exactly what he did want he explained to the girl one time when Robert was out trying to sell a watch he'd lifted from someone's pocket the previous evening.

What he wanted to do was watch. Not openly, not with the boy knowing. Only when they got tight up against one another and the two of them got hot and the boy got hard, then all she had to do was find a way of sliding the thin blanket off the pair of them without Robert realizing.

That was all: that was what the girl did, not minding the harmless old man's snatch of pleasure as Robert spent himself on the dark honeyed skin of her belly.

They would have been there still if Robert hadn't swung his head round too fast and seen the eyes watching them, eager and excited in the close stink of the small room.

It had been all the girl could do to prevent Robert from beating the man to a pulp. And by that time, he was anxious to move on anyway, more and more certain that his mother had lied to him all those years before; all the more certain that his father was alive. Not just alive, but close. He had nothing to go on other than his feelings – until he overheard a woman talking about a drifter she'd run across down Salinas way who'd given her the best time she'd had in years. A good-looking gambler who'd drunk champagne out of her shoe and insisted on lifting her on top of the piano and accompanying himself while he sang a serenade; a lover who had the energy of a man ten, fifteen years his junior and who had the manners to finish last and with a smile still on his face; a man who said his name was Jordan MacPhail.

The girl had wanted to leave the city anyway and she'd persuaded Robert that he ought to head south for Salinas right away; that the two of them ought to go together.

Okay, Robert had agreed, that's what we'll do. But we'll do it right. We'll be ready. So they'd both stolen and hustled as many hours of the day as they could, the girl pulling in as many men as she could and stealing from their pockets even as they were bent drunkenly over her.

When are we leaving? had been her impatient question, morning after morning as Robert counted their stake.

And one more day, one more night, had been his reply.

She saw her escape in sticking with him and waited for him to say the word. If he did, she never heard it. Robert snuck away in the middle of the night and took every cent that they'd scraped together with him. All he left her was a pair of worn-out boots and some extra space on the floor.

Fowler and Hart listened to the story and looked at her, arms resting on the table. In her face a mixture of pride and pain. She was half Apache, half white. Neither wanted her. It was doubtful that she was much more than sixteen years old.

'What'll you do?' Hart asked. 'You goin' to go find him?'

'What for?' she spat back. 'So's he can run out on me

again? Take what I got an' run?' She wiped the back of her arm across her mouth. 'It ain't so great down there anyway. I'm better off stickin' where I am.'

Fowler grunted.

Hart thought of the crib where they'd found her, with the tin bowl and strip of muddy oilcloth and the semen-stained bed; he remembered the dirty rooms and the open cess pools swimming with disease and the naked kids playing in puddles of excrement; remembered the whores' customers in dress suits and the gilt-framed oil paintings and a dinner served on bone china plates and eaten with solid silver knives and forks. He couldn't look the girl in the face any longer. He stood up and went over to the curved bar and drank whisky too fast until Fowler had slipped some of Lydia MacPhail's money into her small brown hand and she'd gone back out into the street.

Still he didn't go back to the table. Not till he'd drunk enough to clear all those things from his mind. Clear them or smear them into such a muddle and mess that he didn't recognize them anyway. Fowler didn't ask him about what he'd been up to, just nodded and tipped the bourbon bottle over his glass and had one more. And one more. And one more. By the time the barman got to wondering if they were intending leaving or simply sliding under the table to be swabbed up in the morning with the vomit and sawdust, both men were only barely able to stand unaided.

The air was surprisingly cold outside and most of the clamour of the night had faded. The street was ridged and uneven and they began to walk downhill, using one another for support, the breeze clearing their minds just enough for them to know which direction they wanted.

Fowler grumbled something about setting out for Salinas at first light and Hart half-thought that was a pretty stupid thing to be saying.

That was when he saw them: strung out across the road from sidewalk to wall. Not moving, simply standing there, hands pushed down into belts or the tops of their pants –

those hands that weren't occupied with other things. The couple of street lights still working picked out young faces, a few beginning to show the first signs of a beard or a thickening of hair across the upper lip. They were not moving. Nonchalant. Light glinting on blade or broken sword, an open razor and the barrel of a gun.

Not moving.

Hart shook Fowler and watched the detective's eyes open and blink and close again as he slumped forward and would have fallen there in the street if Hart hadn't caught him.

Not moving: one of them threw back his head and laughed, high and wild like a young jackal.

Hart turned his head and saw more of them had silently slipped into position behind. Six or seven spread wide in a curve across the street.

Not moving.

'Fowler! Wake the hell up!'

The heavy body shook itself and eyes peered dimly out, vaguely aware now of what was going on.

'Give 'em some money,' said the slurred voice. 'Throw 'em your gun. Maybe they'll let us through.'

'Like hell!'

'What else you goin' to do? Fight 'em all?' Fowler started laughing, lurching away from Hart across the street, arms flapping from his sides. 'Gonna fight 'em all, huh? All these fine young men? That what you're gonna do, huh? Huh?'

Hart gazed at Fowler in disgust till the same boy's laugh slashed across his attention. The larger bunch of them were starting to move slowly forward, the rearguard remaining where they were. He could see their faces more clearly now, see that they ranged in age from sixteen or seventeen down to eleven and twelve. Faces that were thin with hunger and eyes that were mean and old ahead of their time. Twenty yards off now and starting to tighten their formation, closing in. Hart saw a patched leather vest, worn cotton shirts, again the flash of the razor blade and the jagged edge of an old seaman's sword tight in some kid's bony fingers.

‘Give ’em everythin’ you got!’ called Fowler, his drunken body staggering this way and that, haphazardly towards them. ‘Give it to ’em! Every damn thing! Let ’em have it!’

Suddenly he was no longer rolling and his voice was no longer slurred. He straightened and his pistol was clear of his pocket and the first crack of gunfire stopped the gang in its tracks, one of them staggering back with a slug high in his chest.

Hart threw back the Indian blanket and revealed the sawn-off at his belt. The line of kids started yelling and clamouring and rushed towards the two of them. Hart pulled the Meteor up from his belt and rested the barrel over the curve of his left arm. He waited until a bunch of them were no more than ten yards off before squeezing back on the triggers. Ten-gauge shot carved into a welter of arms and legs as from the corner of one eye Hart saw Fowler snap off a couple more shots before pistol-whipping one of the marauding kids to the ground.

Hart tossed the shotgun into his left hand and swerved round in a crouch. The Colt sped into his hand and he dropped two of the rear group and narrowly missed a third before they turned tail and fled up the street.

He sensed someone closing on him fast and swung the shotgun back round, catching the kid along the jawline and splintering the bone. A razor came for his head and he ducked back from its vicious swing, firing the Colt from close range. The impact of the bullet hurled the boy into the air and before he landed in a sprawling heap, Hart had dropped the pistol into its holster and snapped the shotgun open, thumbing fresh shells down into the chambers.

Fowler broke a kid’s arm by slamming the back of the elbow down hard against his thigh and holding on tight. The broken length of sword clattered to the ground and Fowler rolled the youth away and stood straight.

Hart had the shotgun levelled and ready but there wasn’t anyone else to use it on. Apart from the dead and the crying, the street was empty again.

He slotted the weapon back down into his belt and swung the blanket back to cover it. 'Had me fooled good,' he said.

'Meanin' what?'

'Figured you drunk out of your head for sure.'

Fowler shook his bear-like head and growled: 'Drunk! Course I was drunk! You don't reckon I can fight like that when I'm sober, do you?'

Hart shook his head and stepped over a writhing body, following the detective down the hill towards the centre of the city.

The first glimmer of light through the hotel window assaulted his eyes. The space between his head throbbed like a hollow drum and his mouth tasted like a three-month saddle blanket. When anything of any clarity occured to him it was that Fowler woke up in a state like that most mornings of his life: as a thought it wasn't very profound but it gave him a shade of satisfaction.

He washed and dressed slowly, each action as if he were doing it for the first time.

Breakfast was strong black coffee and a piece of dry rye bread that he broke between his fingers and dunked down into the cup.

Fowler sat opposite him and kept counsel with the depths of his beard.

Finally, Hart pushed the cup away, sloshing some of his refill over the table. 'You realize what we done last night?'

Fowler's voice was gruff and careful. 'Sure I know what we done.'

'We killed two, three kids less than sixteen years of age. Maybe more than that. Kids younger'n this one we're supposed to be lookin' for.'

'What was we supposed to do? Pat 'em on the head and drop 'em a dollar?'

'That ain't the same as . . .' Hart stood up sharply and sent more of his coffee flying. It was a considerable effort for Fowler to raise his head high enough to see his face. 'We never tried to talk our way out. Never done nothin' 'cept cut loose and blast 'em with everythin' we had.'

Fowler nodded gravely. 'That's damn right!'

'An' you feel okay 'bout that?'

'Okay? you betcha I feel okay. More'n okay. I feel pretty fuckin' good about it!'

'We . . .'

Fowler jabbed a finger at him. 'We let those punks think they were goin' to walk all over us an' leave us on the street for dead. They'd've stripped every bit of clothin' off our backs and taken our scalps an' hides as well if they reckoned there was any way of sellin' 'em. Those bastards are worse'n vultures on account of they don't wait till the blood's turned cold. There ain't one bit of feelin' left in 'em and they got the whole of Frisco runnin' scared. Runnin' scared and we took 'em, the two of us. Blasted the punk bastards till they couldn't get out of there fast enough. An' we didn't take a scratch either one of us.'

The finger relaxed, 'Don't you waste no sympathy on scum like that, Wes. Just don't, that's all.'

'Damn it, Fowler! They was kids!'

The detective threw back his chair so vehemently it crashed against the back wall, splintering one leg. Everyone else in the dining room was staring at them now, the waitress clutching her apron to her chest and breathing open-mouthed.

'They was killers, Wes. Killers, pure an' simple. You saw 'em. Razors and guns an' every damn weapon you can think of. They'd have cut your throat as soon as spit in your face. You think they'd've felt sorry for that? Think they'd have felt sorry for anythin'?' He gave his head a vigorous shake that made him wince. 'They don't know what feelin' is. Not any longer.'

They did once, Hart was thinking, every one of them.

He didn't say it; he didn't say a thing. Turned on his heel and stomped out into the street and had to shield his eyes against the light. He knew most of what Fowler had said was right, but that still didn't make him forget the momentary look of realization and terror on the face of a boy of no more than fifteen immediately before he'd sent a bullet tearing through his body.

Fowler being right didn't wipe that out, didn't make the whole thing any better. He began to walk down the sidewalk, not really looking where he was going, men and women stepping out of his way rather than argue with his determination or the gun at his side. Half a mile on, he stopped and wiped the sweat that had gathered in the centre of his palms on to the sides of his pants. He knew where he was going and what he was going to do. He was feeling so damned bad that there wasn't anything in that letter that was going to make him feel any worse.

He turned fast and collided with a man who began to complain until he looked into Hart's face and moved on his way with the words frozen in his mouth.

Fowler wasn't downstairs and the door to his room was shut fast. Hart let himself into his own room and tore open the drawer, hurling the spare shirt on to the floor. The writing on the envelope was sharp against his eyes and when he picked it up, the rough paper burned his fingers.

Her eyes were hazel tinged with green; the skin on her arms was warm and smooth and he wanted to feel it against him one more time and knew it was impossible. He searched her face for a sign of tears and found none; his pleading washed back off her like water from the smoothest stone.

Behind them the place he'd built for them to live in, the room at the side for the kid they . . .

The envelope was in half between Hart's calloused fingers. Half and then half again. Again. Again. He tore and ripped until it was no more than flakes of paper that he made into a pile at the bottom of the enamel bowl on the wash stand and watched as the spurt of flame from the match caught and consumed. Bitter and black.

He grabbed his things, checked his weapons, shouldered

open his door and kicked the one to Fowler's hard enough to shake it in the frame.

'You ridin' to Salinas or do I go alone?' Feet crashing down the stairs before the detective had the chance to answer.

Eleven

They came down off the old stage road to Salinas, leaving the Santa Anas over their left shoulder. The valleys were broad and the land good, cottonwoods and pepper trees blotched across it like so many small splashes of darker paint. Indians and Mexicans and the occasional poor white worked the fields, broccoli and beans and fruit and all manner of squash, avocados and oranges. They passed a girl of maybe ten with a herd of off-white and shaggy-bearded Nubian goats, an old man, three-parts blind, hitting the ground with a long stick, moving cattle across a broad swathe of pasture.

They never talked.

Hart kept his thoughts to himself except where his scarcely suppressed anger showed in the lean lines of his face and the bitter blue of his eyes.

Fowler wasn't sure if what the other man was feeling was all due to what had happened back in the city, or whether there was something else he didn't know about. Either way, he wasn't about to ask. Firing questions at Hart in that mood would be like stepping up to a prize bull with your best red shirt on and shackles round your feet. Not that he would have had Hart anywhere else than where he was. Alone in that street the other night, he doubted if he'd have got out alive. No matter how well he tricked them pretending to be drunker than he was, there would have been too many for him. And the way the big man had cut loose with that stashed sawn-off of his was a sight to behold.

He glanced at Hart's face and said a quick prayer for anyone who was unfortunate enough to get on his wrong side that day. All that anger and bitterness building up inside him and how the hell was he about to let it out? If it had been Fowler himself, then a bottle of bourbon would have held most of the answer – but that wouldn't do it for Wes Hart. Didn't seem as though talking would either . . . and sure as hell something had to.

Fowler shook his head and flicked the reins. Other men, he'd have figured it was some kind of woman trouble got him riled up that way. But Wes Hart? He couldn't see that. Couldn't see it at all.

They rode into Salinas from the north-east, letting their mounts walk in slow and easy back of a high-sided wagon loaded to the brim with farm produce and drawn by a team of four overladen mules. There were quite a few folk on the street, some of them stretched out across the boardwalk, hats dipped over their eyes and legs straight. The sun was just shifting over the middle of a clear blue sky and sweat ran down both riders' faces and stuck their clothes to their bodies like a second skin. The horses tossed their heads, flicked their tails at the inevitable flies.

Fowler could feel his thirst building up inside him like a dam about to bust. He drew over towards a sign that said *Livery and Feed* and Hart followed suit.

'Soon as we get the horses settled we'd best split up. Cover things quicker that way. You take whatever's left of the main street, I'll take right. Meet back at the Santa Rita in a couple of hours.'

Hart followed the line from Fowler's finger to the building down the street with a balcony jutting over the sidewalk and a black and white cat sunning itself on the front corner of the rail. One false turn in its sleep and it would topple to the street below . . . except that cats didn't do things like that.

'Okay?'

Hart gave the detective a quick nod and turned on his heels, striding across towards the mid-point between a barber shop and saddler's, hat pulled down at a steep angle over his eyes and the curved fingers of his right hand almost brushing the pearl-handled grip of his gun.

Hart had tried three saloons and the barber shop without much luck. A few folk had heard of a gambler by the name of Jordan MacPhail but didn't know where he'd got to. The man with a runny eye who was swabbing the floor in the California Dream Saloon and Bar thought there'd been a feller called Griff McPeters in town a month or more back, but on further questioning McPeters turned out to be under five foot seven inches tall, almost as wide and the possessor of a fine Scottish accent and a twitch whenever he was winning. The barber paused in stropping his razor long enough to check that Hart wasn't mistaken in the name and didn't really want to find someone called Jerry McCann, who was the sort of man who ought to be run out of town on account of something. It transpired that McCann had recently opened up his own barber shop in Salinas, after working in barbed partnership with his now rival for three years. Hart let the man go back to his strop and declined the offer of a cut-price shave.

'Keep away from that butcher McCann,' the barber called after him. 'He'll give you a cut-throat shave instead!'

Hart moved on to a cantina back from the main street, set down towards a cluster of shacks that marked the Mexican end of town. There was no name above the door, no door in the frame. Flies hummed lazily a couple of inches below the low ceiling. There were maybe a dozen people inside and three-quarters of them asleep, but then it was still siesta time. The woman behind the bar had been pretty just long enough ago for her to remember the way men reacted to her appearance; she saw Hart enter and wondered what a handsome *gringo* was doing walking into her cantina in the middle of the day. Usually they came, when they came at all, when they were too far gone in drink to get served anywhere else in town.

She smiled her once pretty smile and shrugged her left shoulder so that her loose white blouse slid down to show a few inches more plump skin.

'*Señor*?'

Hart pushed the hat brim back and she admired his blue eyes. He said: 'Maybe you can help me?'

She raised an eyebrow and looked a little too obviously at his body, as much to suggest, well, she might, she might.

'I'm lookin' for a man . . .'

She pursed her lips and said nothing, but her eyes were smiling.

'Name of MacPhail.'

She surprised him; she didn't shrug her shoulders to signify the name meant little to her as others had done; she didn't gesture emptily with her hands; neither did she shake her head and say she had never heard of him. What she did was say: 'Jordan MacPhail?'

Hart started. 'You know him?'

'No, *señor*.'

'But you know the name . . .'

'You are not the only one looking for him.'

Then Hart nodded, understanding. 'The boy.'

'*Si*, the boy.'

'When was he here?'

She rubbed her plump fingers over her forearm, thinking. 'Five, six days since.'

'An' you didn't know nothin' 'bout MacPhail?'

She shook her head. 'He said MacPhail was his father.'

'That's what he says.'

'It isn't true?'

'His mother told him his father died. He don't believe it. Don't want to, I guess.'

'A boy, he needs a father.'

Hart nodded. His own father had brought Hart's mother and Hart, quickening inside her belly, over the California Trail to Sacramento. They'd made Sutter's Fort in time for the birth to take place there, his mother nearly dying with the strain of the journey weighing down so heavily upon her. But she'd survived and so had Wes and so, for a time, had his father. But Sutter, instead of striving to keep that part of California independent, had encouraged as many Americans as possible to settle there, the trade filling his pockets times over. Hart's father had sided with the *Californios* and fought to keep the state independent. He had ridden out against General Kearny and not ridden back.

Wes had been three years of age: the same age as young Robert MacPhail when he was told that his father, too, had died.

Hart nodded: he knew all about sons needing their fathers.

Knew, also, about the gut feeling that comes when you're certain he isn't really dead. Even though, in his case, he'd seen the coffin lowered into the ground and heard the cornet and the cannon, seen the flowers and the tears on his mother's face.

Still, he'd lived through his childhood with an expectation always at the back of his mind. One day the door would open and he would walk through, holding out his arms. Or a letter would come from Mexico or some far-off land Hart could only dream about. He had gone to sea on a whaler. Or trekked back over the Sierras and owned a ranch in Montana and any day now he was sending for his son so that they could work it together . . .

Since his mother's remarriage, much of this had been simple wish-fulfilment that would take him out of reach of his step-father's fists when the prospector arrived back from yet another empty journey off into the heart of the mother lode.

When at last he had believed the truth about his father's death, fourteen years of age and with the beginnings of a man about him, he had left home and never returned.

Robert MacPhail was sixteen and still searching, though he'd left home to do it.

'How come you're looking for him too?'

Hart looked at the woman, realizing that she'd spoken, without being certain what she'd said.

'I said, how come you want to find him, this Jordan MacPhail?'

He ignored her question and asked another in its place. 'The kid – he have any friends here? Anyone who might know where he'd gone?'

'I don't know, *señor*. He slept rough, ate what was thrown away behind one place or another. Begged for drinks. He had a little money, but he did not like to spend it. He thought it must last him a long time.'

'An' you don't know where I'll find this Jordan MacPhail?'

She shook her head a little sadly, for she would have liked to have been able to help him, this tall *gringo* with the faded-blue eyes; would have liked to speak with him longer. But there was nothing more to say and Ramon was waiting at the other end of the bar for tequilla.

'Good luck, *señor*. I hope you find him, this man you are searching for.'

She gave him her best smile and walked slowly towards Ramon, who tossed a coin onto the counter and glared at the *gringo*'s back as he stepped through the door.

Fowler had been in the back room of the Santa Ana for long enough to drink three good shots of bourbon and get good and hungry for a steak. As soon as Hart arrived he yelled an order for a couple of t-bone specials and poured himself another drink.

'Take it easy, huh.'

'What d'you mean, take it easy?'

'Next time you walk into trouble I may not be there to pull you through.'

'Yeah, but you will. I already made sure of that. So just relax an' let me drink.'

Hart scraped over a chair and sat down, leaning it back on its hind legs and resting one boot across the corner of the table.

'What you find out?' Fowler asked.

'About Jordan, not a deal. But . . .'

'But they remembered the kid, huh?'

'Yeah, the kid.'

'Uum.' Fowler shifted the bottle far enough for a plate of thick beef to be set down in front of him, another before Hart. They set to and ate for close to ten minutes without speaking. Fowler was in the act of spitting a piece of gristle from his mouth into the palm of his hand when he heard the tapping on the window. He ignored it at first, only turning his head when the sound persisted. The face that peered through the glass was of a young Mexican kid with both front teeth missing and a dark question mark of hair falling down towards the bridge of his nose.

'Got a friend,' Hart commented, cutting through the last couple of inches of meat.

'Yeah. Like my horse's got fleas.'

'Don't you reckon you ought to see what he wants?'

'Maybe what he wants is you?'

'Uh-uh. You're the one he's starin' at.'

Fowler grunted something indecipherable and slammed his knife and fork down on the now empty plate. 'Prob'ly only wants the bone.'

But he was wrong. What the kid wanted was to trade a piece of information he thought might be of interest. Seems he'd run around with Robert MacPhail when he was in Salinas, the pair of them sleeping in the stables a couple of nights, probably rolling the odd drunk together though he didn't go so far as to say so.

'What you got that's worth payin' for?' Fowler growled.

'I know where he has gone, *señor*.'

'Know that, huh?'

'Yes, *señor*.' The kid's dark eyes were wide and expectant

and his hand was already itching as he rubbed it against the worn patch on his knee.

'So why don't I knock it out of you, instead of payin' for it?'

'Because before you could do that, *señor*, I would have run away and then you will not find me. And if you do not find me you will not know where Robert has gone.'

'Where's that?'

The boy laughed and showed his missing teeth and held out his hand.

Fowler grumbled low into his beard and tried the kid with a dime. The kid stared at the coin for a couple of seconds before spitting on it. Fowler laughed then and gave him a dollar piece.

The kid grinned almost from ear to ear and whispered: 'Monterey.'

'Monterey, huh?'

'Yes, *señor*.'

'Why Monterey? He goin' sailin'?

'He looks for his father.'

'Okay. So why look in Monterey?'

'Because that is where his father is.'

'How d'you know?'

'I do not know, *señor*.'

'How does Robert reckon he knows?'

'Somebody tell him.'

'Sure, that much I figured. Who told him?'

The boy's arm snaked out and the palm looked pretty itchy again. Fowler wished every cent he'd given for information was staying in his own pocket. He soothed the kid's itch with another fifty cents and waited for the answer.

'He hear it from the sheriff.'

'How come?'

'That is where Robert's father was staying before he left Salinas, *señor*. In the jail.'

Fowler grunted and thanked the boy and went back to

where Hart was patiently waiting, nursing a beer. 'Let's go see the local law.'

'Trouble?'

'For Jordan MacPhail, maybe.'

'Meanin' what?' Hart downed the beer, stood up, reached his hat from the back of the chair.

'Meanin' that the reason not too many folk got to know much about the disappearing mister MacPhail could be on account of the fact he spent most of his time in town locked up in the hoosegow.'

Sheriff Bob Reinhardt was a man with two wives: it was a subject that was well known to him and tended to prey on his mind some, especially when he'd eaten too much and his insides were playing him tricks. While it was never far from his thoughts, then, it was a secret to both women.

Nora Reinhardt was a strong-minded, strong-bodied woman of middle age who'd met Bob through a mail order catalogue and made him agree to sign a paper stating that half the land they were going to live on and farm in New Mexico was hers by legal right and should remain so, whether their marriage took or it didn't. Nora had been married before and that hadn't lasted more than two years on account of her husband getting bit by a snake in the buttocks and Nora not being able to bite and spit the poison out fast enough. She'd been more than willing but her first husband had been a strongly religious man who'd never take his pants off in front of his wife, not to speak of his long johns, and so even as dire an emergency as a rampant rattler couldn't drive his long-held prudery aside right off. It was only after Nora had first argued with him and then – as he got weaker – all but tore his clothes off him, that she got any kind of agreement.

Of course, it was too late. His fever lasted two days and he died with the look of embarrassment and shame still on his face.

They hadn't had much and what was left Nora sold to pay

the doctor and secure her late husband a decent burial and a solid oak marker with a verse from Revelations carved on it underneath his name.

After seven years of trying to make her own way, she gave in and accepted Bob Reinhardt on the basis of one letter and a rough pencilled self-portrait, both of which proved to be highly inaccurate. Still, Nora gritted her teeth and hoped that the fact that he lacked the accomplishments of spelling or drawing or even plain observation wouldn't mean he possessed no other talents or virtues.

She was wrong.

The ranch made a little money because she worked from dawn to dusk seven days a week and drove the occasional hired hand so hard that every one of 'em quit after as much as a month.

'There you go,' Bob would say from his seat on the small porch, pausing to spit tobacco juice down onto the cabbage plants. 'You can't treat a man like that an' expect him to stay round you.'

Nora ground her teeth hard together and choked back on her words and got on with whatever chore she was tending to. Anything but the most straightforward task seemed to leave Bob either winded or perplexed and he'd often as not leave her to it and go wandering off into the hills with a couple of the dogs and a Sharps over his shoulder. One thing he could do, and she couldn't take that away from him, he could shoot and hunt better than most folk she'd ever known. If they had rabbit or deer or pigeon or anything else more than their six-mile neighbours, it was on account of Bob's skill with a rifle.

In fact he got so darned skilful he took to taking out the occasional animal belonging to a sheepfarm in the valley to the north.

Which was fine until the farmer found out by dint of catching him red-handed, Sharps still warm and the sheep slung over his shoulder, dogs trotting by his side pleased as you like.

Bob Reinhardt reckoned it was time to move on and Nora didn't have it in her to change his mind. She did get him to skin the sheep before he left on their second-best mare, promising to write and send for her as soon as he got himself out of New Mexico and settled somewheres else.

Nora waved him goodbye, sent the following posse in the wrong direction after hiding all evidence of the slaughtered sheep and waited for the letter. After a while she stopped waiting, other than to wish it wouldn't arrive. She found, at last, that she could manage just as well without a husband as she had with one. Better, in that there was one less mouth to feed.

As for Bob, he did what a lot of men on the run from the law do – he became a lawman himself. A display of fancy rifle shooting at the Salinas Valley Fair was enough to have the good citizens of Salinas offering him a sheriff's badge and a near-new jailhouse with ample living accommodation built on the back.

Bob Reinhardt took the badge and a month's salary in advance so's to stock up on ammunition and suchlike and pretty soon decided that his new quarters were so ample they were wasted on one person. Besides, there were socks to be darned and clothes to be washed, the prisoners had to be fed and their beds had to be cleaned up once in a while; he could eat for free at the Santa Ana, but once a week, say, it would be kind of good to sit down to a fresh-cooked stew in his own place.

So Sheriff Bob sat out on the sidewalk alongside the jailhouse entrance and rocked slowly back and forth watched the women sashay back and forth likewise. It wasn't long before he'd picked out Sally Clarke, a spinster of twenty-nine with a thin, kindly face and enough of a swish about her skirts to suggest that given the opportunity she wouldn't be lacking in interest when it came to snuggling down between the sheets – which was something else Bob was missing. Not that Nora had been partial to indulging often, but when she had it had been with the hard-working thoroughness she applied to every task, little or great.

Needless to say, the sheriff didn't tell Sally about Nora, nor did he write to Nora inviting her to what was a quick and cheerful little ceremony on a quiet September Sunday in Salinas. It seemed to be a good arrangement all round: Nora had her own place and worked it hard the way she liked and needed; Sally scrimped and saved and slaved and was content enough to do so; Sheriff Reinhardt got fatter and slower and got off his rocking chair less and less often unless it was to prove yet again that he'd lost none of his skill with that old Sharps.

When Fowler and Hart wandered down the street that afternoon there he was, the chair taking him back and forth, back and forth, hat stuck down almost on top of his face and the sunlight catching the silver of his badge.

'Sheriff.'

Bob Reinhardt steadied the chair to a halt, pushed back his hat and blinked into the light. 'Strangers, ain't you?'

Fowler took his wallet from his pocket, picked a card from the wallet and stuck it into the sheriff's hand. The lawman read it slowly a couple of times, chewing all the while like a reflective steer out on the range. Then he handed the card back and averted his head just far enough so's he could spit down into the dirt without splashing either visitor.

'How 'bout your friend here?' He eyed Hart speculatively, letting his gaze hold on the holstered Colt long enough to figure a man who looked like Hart did likely knew how to use it and use it well.

'He's workin' with me,' said Fowler, pulling at one of the lapels on his creased coat and cursing the heat, 'an' we was wonderin' if you could give us a little help.'

'Help?' blinked Reinhardt, hoping that whatever it was didn't occasion him getting up from his chair and stepping off the porch. Not before evening anyways.

'Information.'

The sheriff shrugged and clicked his tongue lazily against the roof of his mouth. Out behind where the two men were standing a brown dog, not much more than a pup, chased a ginger cat forty yards up the street and then just gave up and sank down in the heat, patting the end of its tail against the packed earth.

'Feller named MacPhail. Jordan MacPhail.'

Reinhardt cleared his throat as if about to spit again, but that proved too much for him, too. He swallowed what saliva he'd dragged up and said, 'What about him?'

'That's what we hoped you'd tell us.'

'How come you want to know? There some bounty or somethin' in this? You fellers ain't chasin' after him for nothin'.'

'He went missing a long time back, lit out on his wife and kid. Now the kid's taken it into his head to go lookin' for him. Run off from home. We figure to track MacPhail down. Find the old man, we'll find the boy.'

Reinhardt shifted a couple of inches in his chair and made it look like some effort. 'Sounds logical.'

Fowler nodded; Hart scuffed his boot in the scattering of loose dust over the hard ground and wished to hell they'd get to the point. Standing out there with the sun beating down on the back of his neck wasn't exactly his favourite way of passing the time.

'So what about him, MacPhail? We heard you arrested him a while back.'

'Sure did. Slapped him back in jail there for ten days.'

It was difficult to imagine Sheriff Bob Reinhardt arresting anyone without they walked over to his porch and gave themselves up. Which, as it turned out, was pretty much what had happened.

Reinhardt set himself rocking and told them what had happened. MacPhail had come to town with an actress named Louise Langrishe, who was due to give a performance at the Salinas Palace Theatre, which was a run-down barn of a building which was used as a warehouse when it wasn't putting on shows. The usual performers they drew to Salinas Valley were fourth-rate stars who'd been booed out of San Francisco and were trying to work their way back east. Either that or young no-hopers who wanted to make a name for themselves and move on to better things.

Miss Langrishe came into the former category. She had acted in the legitimate theatre in Boston and Washington for a number of years, the size of her parts getting smaller as her name appeared lower and lower down on the playbills. Eventually she made the switch to musical comedy, where her figure looked good in a variety of striking gowns but her voice had all the subtlety of a double-edged saw in combat with a redwood.

An engagement in San Francisco proved short-lived and she was rescued from a hail of abuse and rotting tomatoes by a handsome if less than well-dressed gambler who introduced himself as Jordan MacPhail. Louise was eight or nine years older than MacPhail and there was something about his good looks that made her thanks to him rather more lingering than might otherwise have been the case. She made MacPhail her manager and bodyguard and he somehow set up a tour of California for her which was what brought them, by stage, to Salinas.

The local audience were less than delighted by Miss Langrishe's act – a mixture of speeches from *Romeo and Juliet* and *The Taming of the Shrew* and musical comedy songs performed to a less than certain piano accompaniment. It became obvious to MacPhail that the tour was about to sag to a stop and they'd be lucky to get paid for their present engagement. Duly, he pocketed the one half they'd been paid on arrival, helped himself to whatever of Louise stage jewels might find a buyer and slipped out to where he'd left his horse ready and saddled. When he got there he found himself face to face with an enraged Louise, a derringer pistol in her gloved hand. MacPhail tried to grab it from her and she shot him in the ear, taking the lower part clean off. He wasn't about to risk where the second one might go.

Louise marched him over the street to the sheriff's place and demanded that he be thrown into jail. Reinhardt promptly fined him fifty dollars, which he took from the bills he found in his pocket and which represented Miss Langrishe's wages, and locked him up for ten days. On the fourth day Jordan knocked the cell door back into the sheriff's wife's face when she brought him his breakfast, stole the sheriff's best horse and galloped west as fast as he could.

'You set out after him?'

'Sure did. Rounded up a ten-man posse and chased that bastard twenty mile.'

'But you didn't catch him?'

'Only tracks.'

'Headin' which way?'

'Ain't but one place to head an' that's Monterey.'

Fowler nodded and thanked the lawman for his help. Hart asked if he knew anything about a kid in town looking for MacPhail and Reinhardt allowed that he might've heard of someone goin' round askin' questions but he'd never seen hide nor hair of him. Certainly didn't know where he was now.

'Could've spoke with someone else on that posse though, couldn't he?'

'Could.'

'An' they'd've said Monterey, same as you did.'

'Reckon so.'

'Thanks, sheriff. You take it easy now.'

Bob Reinhardt raised a hand in acknowledgement. 'Don't you worry yourself none 'bout that. An' good luck lookin' for . . . lookin' for . . . oh, hell, whatever the feller's name was.'

Fowler shrugged his shoulders and grunted. For a man who'd been shot in the ear by an actress, Jordan MacPhail sure didn't stick in folks' minds for long. But then maybe that kind of thing happened just about every day in a lively place like Salinas.

Hart stepped over the sleeping pup and suggested he step

up the street and check with someone at the Palace if they knew any more about the affair than the sheriff. Fowler agreed and set himself to find the doctor who'd tended to MacPhail's ear and sewn what was left of it back together again.

Less than an hour later they'd succeeded in checking the sheriff's story as far as they were able; nothing new turned up except that Louise Langrishe had lasted another two nights of her engagement before boarding a stage for Los Angeles.

'She'll never make a name for herself in that one-horse town,' growled Fowler. 'Makes Salinas look like San Francisco on a fast night.'

'When we headin' out towards Monterey?' asked Hart.

'Come mornin', I guess. Ain't no point ridin' through the night. If MacPhail's there, he'll likely be there a while longer.'

'An' if the boy's found him?'

'Depends how he reacts. Might not want to see the kid after all this time. Walked out on him, didn't he? Didn't seem too worried about that.'

Sometimes, Hart was thinking, a man walks out on things he'd rather stay around on account of there don't seem any other way to play it.

'Yeah,' he said to Fowler, 'guess he did at that.'

'I'd hate to be that kid if he catches up with his father after all this time an' the man no more'n turns his back on him and tells him he don't want to know.'

Hart nodded his head and eased himself back in the chair where he was watching Fowler make a mess of yet another bottle of bourbon. He was trying to figure out what might pass through MacPhail's mind when a boy came up to him and said he was the son he'd ridden away from thirteen years ago. He wondered how the boy would be feeling at the same moment. Wondered what it would have done to him if instead of being in that coffin, his own father had survived, only to walk back into his life all those years later.

When he didn't want to think about it any more he pulled Fowler's bottle towards him and poured himself a stiff shot.

Monterey would see it over, he guessed, whichever way it jumped.

Twelve

Monterey hung tight to the coast, pressed in by weathered cypresses whose branches hung with fog like old man's beard. Pines pointed the way to the lazy cluster of hills that tumbled back along the peninsula. The waterfront quay stood out of the turning blue of the water on stilts that glowed yellow-red; here and there men sat dangling their legs and fishing. Behind them the warehouses and boat houses fought for space, the rusted iron roof of one angling down against another. Gulls rose and swooped and harried the small fishing boats as they tied up, their screeching greed threatening to cut out all other sound.

'What do we do when we find him?' Hart stood in the temporary shade of the livery door, his grey being led away behind him.

Fowler hunched against the opposite side of the high arch, fumbling inside his pockets for a match to light the short stub of a cigar clamped between his teeth. 'Which?' he muttered. 'The father?'

Hart shook his head. 'The son.'

The match head scraped and spurted and the end of the cigar slowly reddened; Fowler drew hard, coughed, watched as a funnel of soft grey smoke drifted out into the warm air. 'Kinda late to ask, ain't it?'

'Meanin'?'

'Meanin' you ride all this way, all these miles sayin' nothin'.'

Hart shrugged, pushed the heel of his boot hard against the wood at back of him. 'Two reasons I'm here. One, you asked.'

Fowler concentrated on the end of his cigar.

'Two, it's a job. You hired me on. Agency rates. I'm gettin' paid.'

'Then I don't see your problem.'

'Didn't say there was a problem. Just want to know what you got in mind.'

Fowler broke into a sudden laugh which quickly became a splutter; he pulled the cigar clear from his mouth as he half-choked, drew the flask from his pocket and had a quick swig at the bourbon.

'Maybe you should know me better'n to ask that?' There was a smile somewhere around Fowler's eyes, recessed as they were between the folds of flesh screwed together on his face.

'I always thought detectives worked to some kind of plan.'

'You bet! Pick myself up every time I fall down. Other than that, I prefer to take things how they come.'

'An' Robert MacPhail, you plannin' to take him?'

'Let's find him first.'

'But when we do?'

Fowler shook his head slowly. 'Persistent bastard, ain't you?'

'Yeah. When I need to be.'

'All right.' Fowler made a short chopping gesture with his hand. 'His mother wants him back, that's what she's payin' for . . .'

'So you're goin' to drag him across a hundred miles of this damned country . . .'

'Look, you ask a question. At least let me finish tellin' you what you want to know.'

'Okay, only I don't see how . . .'

'I said let me finish!'

'I said okay!'

Both men stared hard at one another. The livery man hovered in the background, wanting to talk to Fowler about payment but figuring now wasn't exactly the best time. He moved into one of the stalls and started tossing some hay around. Fowler had another fast shot from his flask, offering it across the doorway to Hart, who refused with a quick shake of the head.

'We find the kid, I try to persuade him, right. Tell him his ma's missin' him, she's worried about him, why don't he take a couple of weeks out and ride back an' see her, talk with her. After that what he does is up to him.'

Hart breathed heavily, shifting his weight. What Fowler said sounded all too reasonable – he just couldn't see it working out that way.

'You satisfied?'

'Maybe.'

'Grudging sort of a bastard, ain't you?'

Hart shrugged and started to say something but the detective cut across him. 'What did you think? We were goin' to shanghai him and take him back tied down to a mule?'

'I don't know,' Hart murmured.

'No, you don't!'

'I just don't see a kid like this stoppin' to listen while you say all them reasonable things, that's all.'

'You don't, huh? An' that's all that's worryin' you?'

'No.'

'Jesus Christ!' Fowler began reaching for his bourbon again. 'What the hell else is there?'

Hart looked beyond the livery towards the crowded buildings of the small town. 'Somewhere out there there's his father.'

Fowler exhaled slowly, letting his fingers slide away from the sides of the flask. He drew the cigar end from his mouth and dropped it to the ground, grinding down on it with the heel of his boot. 'Yeah,' he breathed, the word little more than a grating hiss of stale air. 'Yeah. Somewhere.'

Jordan MacPhail was sitting on the uneven edge of a bed in the back room of a bar less than two hundred yards from the same livery stable. The place was close enough to the water for the lap and turn of the tide to be heard and felt. The floor seemed to shift in the night like on board ship. Jordan winced at the least movement now with his hand, touching the side of his head. A bruise spread across the swelling, brown darkening to purple, and it didn't matter that he couldn't see it. Feeling it was bad enough. Jordan caught his breath and bit down into his lower lip and gingerly felt the head of the swelling, an egg-shape that was crowned by an inch-long ridge of scab crusty to the touch.

He blinked his eyes awake and turned his head and shoulders with difficulty. The mattress sagged at the centre and the woman had rolled down into the dip, the thin cotton sheet pulled up over her body so that all he could see was one round shoulder and a mass of tangled dark hair.

Jordan blinked some more. If he'd wanted to remember her face he wouldn't have been able. She wasn't a woman he'd been keen to remember, she certainly wasn't the woman who was the cause of the lump on his head – all she had been was the woman who'd rolled his face out of the sawdust on the bar floor and wiped the blood away from his face, finally helped him to stand up and thrown his arm over her shoulder so that she could drag him, with difficulty, to the back room where she slept. And worked. Except that this night she wasn't working. She was being human, she was feeling sorry for some feller she'd only seen a few times and whose face and body set her in mind of a man she might have got married to once . . . if that hadn't been in a dream.

Now she slept on, dreaming other dreams, as Jordan MacPhail found his way to the small wash stand and, cursing softly, poured cold water into the bowl from the cracked jug and, scooped a handful of drowned flies from the surface before splashing the water up into his face as gently as possible.

Behind him the woman stirred and he saw now that her arm was not big but big and fat, that she was fat all over, the sag of her breasts outlined beneath the sheet, the roundness where her hips were somewhere hidden.

He wanted some coffee to break the pain in his head and clear the taste of cheap, warm beer from his mouth. He felt in his pants pocket and was surprised to find the few bills and coins he had left were still there. Quickly, the woman moving again, he looked around the small room, searching for any money she might have hidden. All he found was a twenty-cent piece, which he shook his head at and left where it was.

Jordan winced again, the sudden movement of his head a mistake.

He rested one hand on the head of the bed and tried to drag his thoughts together. The woman he'd been propositioning, the wrong woman, or rather the right woman at the wrong time, she'd been slim and pretty and in the light from the kerosene lamp she'd even been young. She'd played along with him for half an hour or more before the game had started and watched from time to time as he lost more money than he won. When the game broke up, Jordan had made a few suggestions and she'd laughed and told him he was one hell of a feller and then the barkeep had swung some kind of club at his head and he'd gone down and thought for a few seconds about getting back up but the idea never really had one leg, never mind two. He recalled thinking, as he drifted back into unconsciousness, never to try and make out with a bartender's lady again: not when they were in the same bar.

He'd woken up in the small hours to the clamour of gulls and the warmth of a strange woman's back. Woken and laid there thinking about how Robert would be back at the place on the water, waiting. Hell, no, he'd be fast asleep. Wouldn't even know he hadn't come back. And so what if he did? Did he figure he was going to change his life, coming out of the blue the way he had, some strange kid he'd never seen for thirteen years? Walking up to him after tagging him around town for the best part of a day. Right up to him and coming out with it straight: I'm your boy. I'm your son, Robert.

Could have been lying. Could've been anyone. Except for the cold shiver that ran the length of Jordan's back and over his shoulders, down into his fingers till they were gripping ice. For seconds his legs refused to move, even to feel.

'I'm your boy. I'm your son, Robert.'

It had taken a long time for Jordan to say anything. He'd stood there and stared at him, tall for a kid of – what the hell age would he be? – but so skinny you could lose him in a high breeze. Looked as if he hadn't eaten anything but grits for weeks. That face, though. Sure was goin' to be a good-lookin' bastard, that was for certain. Good-lookin' bastard just like his old man.

'C'mon. Robert,' he said finally, clapping an arm round the boy's shoulders and turning him. 'Let's go get us a beer. I guess we got us somethin' to celebrate.'

He bought a couple of beers and watched as Robert got through a plate of stew without even seeming to take breath. He did near the same with some deep-dish apple pie, second helpings as well. Jordan shook his head and sank his beer and took the kid out to the place he was using as a base – just for a few days, just while I look around and put a few things together – which was a disused boathouse reached by means of a long curving walkway that teetered out over the water.

Jordan dragged away one of the two old mattresses he'd optimistically bought and pulled it over by the opposite wall.

'There. Now you got a bed. Roof over your head as well.' He made a little mocking laugh. 'Home from home, boy. Reg'lar home from home.'

Robert had been awake since before dawn. The smell of the ocean, the sounds of the birds and the sense of movement beneath the boards had rocked him out of sleep and woken him to the hardness of his mattress and his loneliness in the room.

He lay there for a few moments, lingering over the realization that he had found his father. Not simply found him, but been accepted by him. There they were, living together, father and son.

Except that his father wasn't there. Not at the moment.

Robert thought that perhaps his father had woken even earlier and was somewhere outside. perhaps walking along the edge of the water, fishing for their breakfast. The air was cold and the light was beginning to spin out around the horizon. Robert shivered in this thin shirt and realized that his father had not been back. So what? A grown man – why shouldn't he be having fun? Likely too worried about his son's reaction to bring a woman back home. Robert laughed: maybe in time they'd both bring their women home together, throw the mattresses back together and have one whale of a time!

Mist grew up the legs supporting the walkway like grey ivy. Robert hurried back inside the boathouse and threw one of his father's coats round his shoulders. His eye caught a coffee pot standing near a small stove. He would make his father coffee for breakfast and see the look of surprise and pleasure on his face when he got home.

What seemed hours later there was a lot of movement along the waterfront and the sun was warm now on the boy's back. He'd drunk the contents of the first pot of coffee and a second had become cold. Fear that his father had run out on him was only knocked aside by the fact that so many of his things were still inside the boathouse.

Robert's mind sank lower and lower as he waited, thinking of what his mother had said to him about his father's accident, trying to figure out why she had lied. Why she hadn't wanted to see him again. Why his father had been content to stay away, make no apparent effort to see him. If he had not run off and begun searching on the basis of a half-heard rumour, they would never have met.

When the boy had almost given up hope, he heard steps at the far end of the spidery walkway and turned to see his father approaching, one hand holding a bag over his shoulder, lips pursed together as he shrilly whistled.

'Robert!'

Robert ignored the greeting, stared at his father accusingly.

'You had breakfast?' Jordan said, choosing to ignore the look and going on past towards the entrance to the boat house. 'Bought a few things.'

He drew bacon and flour and eggs and a fresh-baked loaf of bread from the bag and set them on the square table someone had thrown away under the stilts of the walkway and which he washed down and dragged up – the same way he'd got hold of most of the possessions in the place.

'I said, you had your breakfast?'

'Uh-uh.' Robert shook his head. He was staring at the swelling and the dark bruise back past his father's right eye. 'What in hell's name happened to you?'

Jordan touched the scab and laughed. 'That's a tale, son! That sure is a tale. Wait while I cook up some grub here an' maybe I'll tell it you. Maybe I'll tell you a mess of things.'

He turned away, reaching for the blackened pan. That's what it'll be, he was thinking, so long as I cut it close to the truth – a mess of things.

Thirteen

Since arriving in Monterey Jordan MacPhail hadn't kept his attentions to the girl of a barkeep in a waterfront bar. Better for him if he had. That way the only trouble that would have come his way would have been a two-day headache, a six-day bruise and a dent in a not inconsiderable ego.

But Jordan had used his charm and looks on women for so long, it was automatic. Except for the fact that he'd never made a woman get out on the streets or into a cathouse on his behalf, he was as close to being a pimp as you can get. Even when he was married to Lydia MacPhail and her gold, he was close to being a pimp. Times he collected the money she deposited in his account at the bank he was as close as a man can be.

The money was never enough on account of Jordan liked to gamble but he wasn't very good at it, didn't even come out a winner when he was using his own marked deck. So Lydia's money paid his bills and let him hold his head up when he walked over to a poker game and asked to sit in.

Another woman's money and other men's women – that was pretty much Jordan's life.

One night in Monterey he'd had more luck than usual at five card stud and an hour of blackjack had confirmed that things were swinging his way at last. Not wanting to miss out while he had the chance, Jordan asked where he could find the biggest game in town and was pointed in the direction of the Spanish Star.

The Star was a gambling place and dance hall that swung out over the ocean at the northernmost edge of town. Lamps hung outside, shifting a little in the wind that slid up off the ocean, and music with a Mexican tinge drifted through the low, white fog along the boardwalk.

The Spanish Star was owned by a Mexican named Luis Aragon and if it had been the only property he owned, he would still have been a wealthy man. Luis took a twenty per cent rake-off from all the tables and the wheel, clipped twenty-five per cent of the bar takings, twenty-five per cent of the girls and he made sure all the liquor that was sold there was stuff he'd freighted in himself.

That would have made Luis Aragon rich.

The other three smaller saloons he owned, the whorehouse he was part-owner of, the thirteen fishing boats and the wine import-export firm he ran made him richer.

Velma Moriarty made him happy. She was twenty-six years old, weighed just enough to move the scales at all, and was a couple of inches taller than average. She got her temper from her Irish father and her round and dark good looks from her Greek mother. When she first met Luis she was working at the whorehouse he owned half of and he almost failed to notice her. Someone pointed out to Velma who the man with the white suit and the dark moustache was and she got close enough to spill a glass of cheap wine in his lap and make it look like it was his fault.

Velma fluttered her eyelids some and wiped Luis down, not letting that opportunity go to waste for a moment. Her hands sent messages up Luis' spine that a straw man would have found hard to ignore.

'What was in your glass?' he asked, struggling to keep calm.

'Champagne,' she said, letting the tip of her tongue rest wetly on the centre of her bottom lip for longer than was strictly necessary.

Luis Aragon smiled and ordered a bottle of champagne. He knew that what she'd been drinking had been ordinary white wine, knew that she had arranged to bump into him on purpose. He thought she had a lot of spunk for a three-dollar whore . . . and his body wasn't forgetting the rubbing down she'd given it.

They sat and talked for hours until the band had stopped playing and then Luis had her driven in his carriage back to the Spanish Star where the music went on until the dawn.

Before the musicians had broken off to eat breakfast, Luis had told Velma she wasn't turning any more three-dollar tricks, she wasn't wasting herself on any other men, she was going to be his mistress.

Velma sat back and surveyed the fifty-year-old paunchy man with thinning hair who now had wine stains on the jacket of his white suit and said that suited her fine.

So it did until Jordan MacPhail chanced to come to the Star looking for a big game of stud and she started feeling a little itch somewhere she hadn't felt it for some time.

Jordan lost most of the money he'd won earlier but when he saw the amount of attention that thin good-looking girl was giving him he reckoned his luck hadn't run out on him at all.

If he'd seen Luis Aragon spying on the two of them round back of the place that night, he might have thought different. Instead, he soothed Velma's itch for a while and kissed her softly on the mouth before slipping back to his houseboat and promising to come calling again.

Time passed like time does and Jordan never got to go back to the Spanish Star and if he had he might not have recognized Velma Moriarty on account of the cut that Luis had razored down the centre of her face. In any case, Velma didn't step out in public that much any more.

Then Robert arrived and moved in with Jordan and if he had any lingering memories of a half-way exciting fifteen minutes pushed up against the back of a building with music throbbing through the wall, they soon slipped away.

Not so for Luis. He'd needed to deal with Velma himself, show her who was boss in his own way – but the cheap gambler she'd betrayed him with, he wasn't worth taking risks over. Not in person. Luis was patient enough to send for two men who would deal with the gambler just like they were sweeping up horse shit from the middle of main street.

*

'Sure I seen him around.' The dealer leaned back in his chair, angling his head round towards Fowler while never taking his eyes off the table. 'He comes in every coupla days, talks a lot, looks real handsome till he sits down and starts playin' the cards.'

The dealer flicked two cards down and with absolute precision against the stack of coins opposite; he gave one new card to the next player in line, then two, then three, took one himself. The deck touched the surface of the table with a soft slap.

'He ain't as good as he thinks he is. He ain't bad . . . but he ain't good. You understand me?'

Fowler grunted: he understood.

'And . . .'

'Yeah?'

'If he could stop his eyes wanderin' off the game an' on to every woman that comes by, he might be a sight better.' The dealer winked without seeming to move the muscles on his face. 'You understand me?'

Wes Hart was sitting on a stool at the end of the downstairs bar at the Spanish Star. He was nursing a glass of beer and trying to hold the barman's attention while other, thirstier, customers called their orders and tapped coins on the brittle counter top.

'. . . so I was saying, he didn't come in here only the once, well, he could've been in other times when I wasn't workin', that'd be Sundays or every other Tuesday, or he could've missed this part of the place altogether, although that'd be strange . . .

He shuffled sideways away to serve a customer, more of a dance than a walk, a clean white towel thrown with studied negligence over his left arm. Hart gave the beer another chance and figured that if he had a free choice of places to drink in the Spanish Star wouldn't rate high. It looked expensive and fake and he figured it might be more acceptable in somewhere like San Francisco than in a fishing town like

Monterey. There had to be more people around with money to throw away than he'd figured. And whoever owned the Star was scooping up most of it.

'. . . anyway, this one time he was here, if it was the one time, he had a couple of drinks and went over to where the big game was, that's up there on the balcony at the back of the room, and he hung around for a while till Mister Aragon, he owns the whole place, he tells him to pull in a chair and . . .'

This time he didn't break off to serve a customer. He stopped in his tracks and stood back from the bar as a side door opened and a Mexican came through, pushing a girl before him. The Mexican was in his fifties and looked pretty good in a white suit and a black hat with a white satin headband. A ring on the small finger of his left hand shone deep like a ruby, which was probably what it was. The pants would have had to be specially tailored to keep his gut in the way they almost did.

The girl was tall and thin; she wasn't so young but she was pretty until she lowered her hand away from her face and showed a scar, deep and dark and right down through the middle of both lips. Her eyes focused on Hart's for a moment and they looked dead.

Maybe she wished the rest of her was too.

The Mexican continued to push her in front of him like a reluctant child and only stopped when they reached an alcove table close by the front door. There were two men already there and they nodded at the man in the white suit and gestured that he should sit down. He did and the girl didn't. Instead she took up her position at the back of his chair, slightly to her right, one of her hands resting lightly on his shoulder, precisely where he'd told her to place it before they'd come in.

'That's him,' breathed the bartender hastily, 'that's Mister Aragon.'

And then he was gone down the bar, setting up drinks with a quicker, more agitated pace.

'Take it easy,' said Hart when he came back.

'Mister Aragon, he doesn't like people talking about him. Not them who work for him.'

'Then maybe he shouldn't walk around in a white suit.'

The bartender looked at Hart as if he'd said something close to blasphemy and backed off. This time one of Hart's hands restrained him, fingers tight and hard through the white towel.

'Finish the story.'

'I got work down the bar.' Fear flashed across his eyes.

'You got work here. Give me a shot of whisky an' get on with what you're sayin'.'

'Well, this feller you're askin' about, he sits in on the game for a couple of hours an' it's getting late and people start drifting home, although the bands still playin' like it will do all night and there ain't no sign of the game breakin' up. Maybe he's winning, maybe he's losing, I don't know, but he's playing.' He paused to gulp down a little air and glance over his shoulder. 'That's when she comes in, Velma.' Another glance, quicker than the first, over the shoulder. 'Her an' this feller, this MacPhail, they start makin' eyes at each other like the moon's full and the band's playin' a seranade instead of some Mexican polka. When MacPhail cuts out of the game, he comes down here and orders a drink, a tequila. He ain't got time to drink it when she's at his shoulder and they're talkin' close. Not long, maybe five minutes, but from the look on his face whatever she's sayin' makes him feel plenty hot an' plenty good. Velma goes back to the table and hangs around Mister Aragon, MacPhail goes out. I figure that's it.'

Someone down the bar yelled for some attention and Hart shot him a look that changed his mind about the kind of hurry he was in.

'I don't know exactly what happened after that, except that somehow they're both together round the back, Velma and MacPhail and whatever they're doin' there it ain't just greetin' the dawn. There's all kinds of commotion and shoutin' and then Velma's runnin' in here till she trips an' falls on the floor, smack in the middle of all the tables. Her dress is torn an' dirty down the back and there's blood all over her hands an' face an' at first I figure she's got a punch on the nose, but that ain't it.' He shook his head with a mixture of sadness and fear. 'That ain't it at all.'

'He did it to her, the feller in white?'

The bartender nodded, retreating slowly.

'And MacPhail? What about MacPhail?'

But he'd gone and was concentrating hard on the tequila bottle he was pouring from. Hart didn't think he'd get him to say any more without pushing the barrel of his Colt into his ribs and that would cause more trouble than he wanted to stir up right then. If Aragon had taken his revenge on his woman, then he wouldn't have let MacPhail off free.

That seemed to leave three possibilities: MacPhail was dead and left on the outskirts of Monterey for the vultures to pick over his bones; he'd had the good sense to clear out as fast as he could; he was still around and Aragon was taking his time in settling their account.

Hart pushed himself down from the stool and took a slow walk down the bar; he was curious to get another look at Luis Aragon and Velma, but also he was interested in the men Aragon was talking to.

When he saw them close-up he was even more interested. He pushed through the doors and out on to the wharf and set out to meet Fowler.

The silver flask glinted in the light of the sun that was bright enough to be near to silver itself. In the distance, back of where Fowler was leaning over the railing, a rectangular boathouse with a steeply sloping roof stood out like a black cut-out against the sea. Silver ripples sprayed up against the legs of the walkway which was little more than a squared-off spiders web linking the boathouse with the land.

Fowler waited until Hart was almost upon him before

taking a last swig and stoppering the flask. He patted it affectionately and dropped it down into his pocket.

Hart wondered what had put the detective in such a good mood.

'Found him?' he asked, taking off his hat just long enough to wipe the rim of sweat from his forehead with the already damp sleeve of his shirt.

'Maybe.' Fowler's eyes twinkled deep in his face. 'How 'bout you?'

Hart told him what he'd learnt at the Spanish Star.

'Don't let up, does he? Our friend Jordan MacPhail.'

'No. An' neither does this Aragon the way I heard it.'

'Yeah.' Fowler scowled at the prospect of some new difficulty butting in when everything seemed on the point of being settled pretty easily. 'Tell me about them two fellers again.'

'One was Mex. Skin more olive than brown. Small features and small bones, I'd guess he weren't more'n a hundred an' twenty, thirty pounds. Seven or so inches above five foot. Wearin' a yellow tan vest with a couple of them concho things sewn on it. Tan pants an' boots with gold spurs. Had some sort of pistol holstered to the right, couldn't make out what.

'Other one was American. Ten years older, taller, beefy-lookin' without a trace of fat. Had a fist wrapped round his glass like he could lose the damn thing from sight just by shiftin' his fingers a little. He had a Smith and Wesson in a holster down by his left leg, knife big enough to butcher a steer with across from it in a plain leather sheath. Oh, yeah, he had somethin' wrong with his face . . . here . . .' Hart touched his left cheek, immediately under the jutting cheek bone. '. . . Looked like it was sort of dead skin. I don't know.'

'Saw all that walkin' by?' Fowler's expression was one of admiration.

'Hung around the bottom end of the bar a little.' He shrugged.

'Ought to be a detective.'

'I don't think so.'

'What's the matter, you don't like the pay?'

'Pay's fine. It was more the company I was thinkin' of.'

Fowler shook his head and automatically pulled out his flask. When Hart declined, he took a swallow, then another and said: 'Feller with the face. He goes by the name of Oklahoma. Like you said, the skin's dead down that side. Got cut up in a fight an' never grew again. Not properly. Look at it close, you can see where the blade went in, right along the contour of the bone.'

'How come you know so much about him?'

Fowler took another shot of bourbon and the flask rattled as though it was close to empty. 'I did it.'

'You did?'

'Sure. Over in Folsom. Feller I was tailin' went through the back of one saloon, in through the front of another. I went after him and he weren't alone. Oklahoma was with him. What happened exactly don't matter, 'cept that there was a struggle an' I got that butcher knife out of his belt and sliced him with it. While that was goin' down, the man I was after cut the traces on my horse, rode his own out of there so fast it took me a week to catch up to him again.'

'And Oklahoma?'

'Looked awful bloody last sight I got of him.'

Hart shook his head ruefully. 'He wouldn't be like to forget you, I guess?'

Fowler found a smile from somewhere. 'Guess not.'

'Makes it a mite difficult, don't it?'

'Could do. Only . . .'

'Only what?'

'We know where MacPhail is an' maybe Oklahoma don't. That is if what we're thinkin' is right and this Aragon's sent for Oklahoma an' his friend to teach MacPhail a lesson he'll carry to the grave.'

'They wasn't just passin' the time of day.'

Fowler spat and narrowly missed the head of a drifting gull. 'I believe it.'

Hart sighed and said: 'How close is MacPhail?'

Fowler grinned and let the flask be long enough to point along the wharf rail, out towards the dark outline of the boathouse that was trapped between the ocean and the spindly web of walkway leading out over the kelp and whitened stones that had been uncovered by the tide.

Fourteen

Jordan and Robert MacPhail were sitting at the far end of the jetty, beyond the boathouse. They were hanging their legs towards the water and their mouths were running greasy with the fat from the bacon they'd cooked up for their first meal together. Whatever time they'd had since Robert had found his father, they'd never got around to sitting down and eating – not at the same time.

It tasted good.

Robert wiped off one side of his mouth and drank some of the bitter coffee, twice as strong for being reheated more than it should. His father was drinking beer from a glazed stone bottle, which he jerked away from his mouth every once in a while to belch loudly. He seemed to think that was a deal of fun and laughed a lot, so Robert, although he figured it was a kind of stupid thing for a grown man to be doing, laughed as well. Maybe his pa was doing it to make him feel at home or something. Maybe he just didn't know how to react.

Robert could understand that.

He didn't know how to behave himself; didn't know what to say. He'd tried asking his father a couple of times what had happened back when he, Robert, had been three and his father had disappeared. What had he done? Where'd he gone? And why had his mother lied the way she had?

But Jordan either didn't hear or he didn't want to talk about it, so all Robert got were blank looks and a turning of the head and another damn belch.

Later, when his father was more used to the idea of him being around, that was when he'd tell him.

The other thing Robert had tried to find out was what his father did to earn money. It wasn't a hell-hole like Frisco where everyone was beggin' and stealin' from everyone else, most folk here seemed to hold down some job of work. They fished or they mended nets and boats, they worked the land in the valley, hell, they did something!

His father, he . . .

Jordan MacPhail farted as a change from belching and winked at Robert. 'Bet that's one thing your ma don't let you do back home, huh?'

Robert nodded a little gravely. She sure as hell did not.

Jordan laughed: 'When you get back to her, you . . .'

'What?'

'I said . . .'

'You said when I get back to her.'

'Sure. When you get back home . . .'

'What home? What damn home?'

'Your home. Your home with her. That goddamn mansion stuck up in the hills. That's where.'

'That ain't my home. My home's where you are. Here.'

'I ain't fixin' to stay . . .'

'Then wherever you go.'

'Look, kid . . .'

'Robert! Call me Robert for fuck's sake! You forgot my name already?'

Jordan reached out a hand and let it fall; Robert sprang to

his feet, spilling what remained of the coffee on to his bare toes. He took a pace towards the boathouse and stopped short.

'You expectin' company?'

'What sort of company?'

'There's a couple of men walking this way.'

'You sure?' Jordan pushed himself to his feet and stood alongside his son. His question didn't need any other answer. Two men, right enough, striding along the narrow walkway like they meant business.

'Get inside.'

'You know 'em, pa?'

'Inside!'

Jordan hustled Robert through the side door and told him to keep out of sight. He lifted up a length of tarpaulin and took a pistol from underneath. Checked that there were five loads in the chamber. He gave Robert one last warning glance, stuck the pistol down into his belt and went to the small, square window at the front. He wiped a circle through the dust and dirt big enough for him to peer out.

They'd passed the angle of the jetty and had no more than twenty yards to come. The one on Jordan's right as they walked was over six foot, a flat-crowned, flat-brimmed hat angled across his eyes so that it dipped a little above his right eye. He let the curve of his fingers pass within inches of the gun that was holstered at his right side. His eyes seemed to be staring directly at the window, directly at Jordan MacPhail's staring eye.

The man alongside him was a head shorter, possibly more. He was wearing badly creased and baggy black pants, a white shirt and a black vest. He had a heavy dark beard and moustache and his eyes seemed almost to have disappeared into the centre of his face. Over his heart he wore a shoulder rig with what looked to be a .44 inside.

Jordan licked his lips, his mouth dry as all hell despite the fact that he'd been swigging back beer for the past hour. All he could taste was that goddamn salt bacon and something he had no difficulty in recognizing as fear. He pulled finger and thumb down over his top lip, rubbed the knuckle of his forefinger back and forth across the bottom of his mouth.

Ten yards out and they'd stopped walking, were quite still, looking at the boathouse as if waiting for him to come out. He could see that the tall one's eyes were pale blue. It wasn't him that spoke.

'Jordan MacPhail! Want to talk with you!'

The words spilled either way across the ocean.

Jordan fingered his gun. If they were from Luis Aragon he didn't stand much of a chance anyway. He'd heard that Aragon had sworn to settle with him for messing with his woman; heard, too, how he'd exacted his revenge on her. He drew the pistol a few inches up from his belt then slid it back down.

What if they weren't from Aragon? What if . . . ?

'We know you're in there. Why'n't you come out an' talk? We don't mean no trouble.'

The voice was low and gruff, as if it came from a throat as dry as Jordan's felt right then.

Jordan watched as the shorter man ostentatiously lifted his hand well clear of his weapon, to show the truth of what he'd said. His companion did the same, hooking his thumb into the centre of his belt, the rest of the hand covering the buckle. Jordan knew that didn't matter a two-cent damn. If they were Aragon's hired guns, they still be able to draw and shoot faster'n he could squeeze off a shot with his gun already out.

'Come on out, MacPhail! We're kinda anxious to talk.'

Jordan sweated on to the grip of his gun. He glanced at Robert, the kid watching anxiously to see how his father was going to play this thing. Great! thought MacPhail. He wants me to show what kind of man I am. Wants me to be a hero and go stridin' out there and get my face shot off!

Jordan wiped his palm down the side of his pants, opened the door and stepped out. Not because he wanted his son to think him brave – simply because there didn't seem to be anything else for him to do.

The wind took the door and slammed it shut behind him and for a split second Jordan thought he'd been shot. His eyes blinked closed and his breath caught and his right hand froze on the grip of his gun. But nothing hammered into him with an unbelievable force and he wasn't hurled back against the boathouse door. He looked at the two strangers and both of their weapons were still holstered; neither their positions nor their expressions had changed.

'You Jordan MacPhail?' It was still the shorter man doing the talking. The other one simply stood and stared and looked almighty dangerous.

'Sure. Sure.'

'Names Fowler. I'm with the Didion Detective Agency.'

Relief oozed from the pores of Jordan's skin for as long as it took him to figure that someone out of his past could've sent this pair after him. It wasn't Luis Aragon's way, but there'd been others with cause enough.

'Your wife sent me . . .'

'I ain't got no wife.'

'That's not the way a judge would see it, but it isn't important either. You see, she wants the boy back.'

'The boy? You mean Robert . . . ?' His face began to burn back in the direction of the boathouse and then he caught himself.

'It's okay,' said Hart, speaking for the first time. 'We know he's there.'

'Then why . . . ?'

'We figured it'd be easier to talk to you first. You might not see to lettin' the boy go.'

'That's up to him, I should've thought.'

Fowler shrugged. Hart looked meaningfuly at the gun sticking up from MacPhail's belt and said: 'Expectin' trouble?'

Jordan blinked. 'What d'you mean, trouble?'

'You was lookin' kinda anxious.'

'I ain't got nothin' to be anxious about.'

Fowler laughed low in his throat. 'That ain't what we heard.'

Jordan's mouth hung open. He felt a pain under his heart that had no perceptible cause. Before he could gulp down some air, the boathouse door had opened and Robert MacPhail had come out on to the boards of the jetty. He was backed up against the rail, closer to Hart than Fowler, closer to his father than either of them. His hair looked several shades lighter with the sun back of it and the same sun glinted off the barrel of the rifle he held against his side with both hands.

'Tale it easy, son,' said Hart, looking towards him and figuring that if it came to a showdown he could safely leave the father to Fowler.

'I'm good an' easy and don't call me son!'

'Okay, Robert. An' I'm glad to hear you're relaxed enough not to let your finger slip against that trigger.'

'I used a gun before,' Robert snarled, throwing up the top corner of his upper lip.

'I'm sure you did.'

'I heard what you said,' Robert called across to Fowler. 'An' none of you sons-of-bitches is takin' me anywhere. Least of all back to her.'

'Her?' echoed Fowler.

'My mother.'

'What's wrong with her, kid?' asked Fowler.

The rifle jerked forward from his side. 'Don't call me . . .'

'I know.' Fowler spread both hands in a gesture that was intended to calm him down. 'Don't call you kid.'

'Anyway, I ain't goin'. I'm stayin' with my pa.'

Hart looked over at Jordan. 'He know that?'

' 'Course he knows! What the hell you think's goin' on here?'

'Ain't what I think that matters. More what your pa there thinks. An' I don't reckon he's so all-fired certain as you are.'

'The hell you don't!'

'You looked in his face lately?'

Instinctively, Jordan MacPhail turned his head away so that Robert couldn't have seen his expression if he'd wanted to. 'The boy's right,' he said. 'Robert's right. Course we're goin' to stay together. Only right ain't it? He says he wants to stay with me instead of go back to her I can understand that.'

Hart wondered why it was suddenly so all right for them to be together when it didn't seem to have bothered Jordan MacPhail for the past thirteen years.

He didn't say so. Fowler said: 'She fixin' to pay him to stay away as well?'

The question stung Jordan like a slap around the face. Robert lowered the rifle some and took a couple of paces across the jetty towards his father.

'What's he mean?'

'Nothin'. Nothin'.'

'Your ma paid money into an account in San Francisco to keep him from comin' back, either to you or her. Every couple of months, regular. For all I know she still does.'

Jordan flushed and he tried again to avoid his son's accusing stare but he could not. He couldn't say anything either. Robert read the truth in his face and went sick in his stomach.

'How much, pa? How much did it take to keep you from comin' home? How damned much? I'll bet one thing, it didn't take a lot. I wasn't worth a lot to you, was I? A hundred dollars a month? Fifty? Twenty-five? Ten? Was that it, pa, ten miserable fuckin' dollars to stay clear of your own son!'

Robert pulled up the rifle and for a moment all three watching, Jordan included, thought he was going to fire it at his father from point bank range. Instead he lifted it high over his head, gave one wild swing and sent it sailing out over the water.

Before it had splashed down, Fowler had started to say, 'Shouldn't have done that, Robert. Rifle might've come in handy.'

The others turned and followed his gaze. Two more men had arrived at the far end of the walkway, one American, one Mexican, both armed and professional, eager to finish off their contract to eliminate Jordan MacPhail with as little fuss as possible.

Fear replaced confusion in Jordan MacPhail's face and his son read it there as clearly as he could have read his own reflection in the water.

'Who are they?' His face thrust towards his father's.

Jordan gulped air and half pushed the boy aside. He looked at Fowler and Hart and then down along the jetty to where Oklahoma and Angel Montero were walking with an almost casual ease.

'Who are they?' Robert grabbed hold of the side of Jordan's shirt and his father knocked his hand away.

'They from Aragon?' Jordan demanded of Fowler.

'Looks that way.'

'You know them?'

'One. That's bad enough.'

Jordan pulled compulsively at his top lip, blinking the sweat from his eyes. 'Help me! Help me and I'll send the boy back! I promise you. Back to his mother. Right off. Only . . . only . . . just help me.'

Robert MacPhail clung to the rail in disgust. His heart was accelerating fast and he didn't want to believe what he'd just heard but there wasn't any way of avoiding it.

'You bastard!' He launched himself off the rail towards his father, fists aiming for his face. 'I ain't no one for you to send anywhere! You stinkin' bas . . .'

Jordan stepped sideways and punched his son in the side of the neck and the boy went down on one knee, gasping for breath. 'Anyone's a bastard round here, kid, I reckon you got a better shot at it than anyone else!'

'Jesus Christ!' hissed Fowler and ground his finger ends hard into the palm of his hands.

Hart fought to keep himself from throwing MacPhail into the water.

'You gonna help me?' Jordan screamed. 'I'll pay you. Anything you ask. Just for God's sake help me!' He pulled at Fowler's arm and tried to spin him round. 'For Christ's sake, she was only a woman!'

'Yeah,' growled Fowler, 'like that was only a kid!'

He flung MacPhail from him like he was clearing shit from his clothing.

Hart watched MacPhail stumble and fall and made no attempt to save him.

Fowler said to Hart: 'Much as we might not want to be involved in this we don't get a lot of choice.'

'He goin' to recognize you?'

Fowler laughed low in his throat, more a growl than a laugh. 'Wouldn't you recognize a man who cut open half your face?'

Hart grinned a shade ruefully and stood wide and a few paces forward, widening the angle. Fowler moved towards the opposite side of the rail, letting his hand drift up towards the shoulder rig that held his Smith and Wesson. MacPhail was still crouched on the boards, his pistol still pushed down into the top of his pants. Robert leaned against the front of the boathouse, watching and not knowing what he wanted to do – even if he could have done anything.

Oklahoma and Angel Montero held their ground some fifteen yards back and the narrowness of the walkway didn't allow them a deal of room.

Oklahoma was staring at Fowler and the side of his face that could smile was making a meal of it.

'See that feller there?' he said to Angel. 'The short, fat guy with the beard. Name's Fowler.' He spat out into the ocean. 'Tell you three things about him. One, he's a detective. Two, he's likely holdin' on to that rail 'cause most of the time he's fallin-down drunk. An three, he's the bastard who ripped up my face and left me with this patch of skin that's deader'n he's goin' to be any minute now.'

Angel pursed his lips and edged his hand an inch or so closer to his gun.

'Which is MacPhail?' asked the Mexican.

'There on the floor,' sneered Oklahoma, 'with the yellow streak down his back.'

Angel smiled and nodded: the conchos on his vest shimmered in the bright light.

'How 'bout you, feller?' Oklahoma gazed at Hart, taking in the Colt Peacemaker at his hip, the pearl-handed butt close to the curled fingers of his calloused hand. 'You want a hand in this or don't you?'

'I got a choice?'

'Sure you got a choice,' Oklahoma smiled. 'You ain't interested in buttin' in on account of that miserable scum down there or mister detective here, you can drop that fancy gun nice as you please an' walk on out. We ain't got no quarrel with you.

Hart stood there giving the matter some thought.

'What about the boy?' Fowler asked.

Oklahoma shook his head. 'I don't give a fuck for the boy.'

'He can go free?' asked Hart.

'Kid!' called Angel, 'Clear out of here. Run past us, jump into the ocean. Go!'

Robert stayed rooted to the spot.

'Okay,' said Hart. 'It ain't my fight. None of it.'

Oklahoma smiled and nodded as Hart used the forefinger and thumb of his left hand to gently lift the Colt from his holster and lower it to the boards. He could see the white foam riding the waves through the gaps in the jetty. When he straightened up he swung his head round towards Robert MacPhail and said: 'You coming?'

Robert glared at him hard: 'I'm findin' out just how many cowards there are in this damn world!'

He spoke to Hart but the words were meant for his father.

It was clear from the look on Jordan's face that he knew. Hart shrugged and kicked the gun sideways a couple of feet, then began slowly to walk towards the two gunmen.

Without seeming to have made any movement, Angel's gun was in his hand and he was pointing it at Hart. 'No chances,' he said, smiling with a mouthful of even teeth.

Oklahoma laughed and looked first at Fowler and then Jordan MacPhail. 'Yeah,' he said, 'just like these two.'

A gull squawked and glided close overhead. Hart stepped right up to the Mexican's gun, right past the small, dark hole at the barrel's end, passing between Angel and Oklahoma without quite touching either.

'Some friends you got, Fowler,' leered Oklahoma and started to move towards his gun.

Hart slipped on the damp boards and his legs gave beneath him, except that he wasn't slipping. His fingers closed on the shaft of the knife inside his boot and it came slashing up even as Angel turned. The point of the blade pierced the flesh underneath the elbow of his gun arm and cut up and through. Skin folded back and blood leapt as Hart removed the best part of Angel's middle finger and knocked the pistol high into the air.

Close alongside, Oklahoma's immediate reaction was to turn towards the sudden movement, bringing his half-drawn gun round with him. Almost there, he realized he was wrong but then it was too late. Fowler's Smith and Wesson was pushed out towards him and the hammer clicked back clean and smooth. The first shot shattered the bone at the top of Oklahoma's left shoulder and caused him to loose hold on his gun. The second smashed his left knee cap and toppled him to the floor with a grinding scream.

Hart had Angel's bleeding arm high behind his back and his handsome nose against one of the boards of the jetty. The barrel of Angel's own pistol was cold against the olive skin at the nape of his neck.

Hart and Fowler exchanged glances, smiles even.

'You had enough?' Hart asked Angel.

The Mexican grunted something that could have been yes or could have been no. Hart raised the Colt back high enough to slam it down against Angel's head with the force to bust his nose on the board beneath his face.

Fowler reached down and slid Oklahoma's knife out of its sheath and pressed the flat of the blade against the dead skin of his cheek. 'Is it true, you ain't got no feelin' there?' he asked with a throaty chuckle that broke and faded fast. 'You were fixin' to kill me, you bastard!'

He turned the blade and drew a line diagonally through the patch of skin, watching the blood slowly bubble up, watching Oklahoma's eyes fill with hate and nothing more.

'That's the truth,' announced Fowler, standing up. 'Don't feel a damn thing.'

He tossed the knife down into the ocean and watched it disappear from sight.

'Reckon these two'll be any more trouble?' asked Fowler.

'Not till a few bits and pieces done mended,' replied Hart. 'By which time Luis Aragon may have someone on their tail for messin' this whole thing up.'

Jordan MacPhail, surprised at finding himself still alive, was walking towards them with no clear idea of what he wanted to say. Neither Fowler nor Hart had a damn thing they wanted to say to him. Both men turned their back towards him and began to walk along the walkway, side by side.

Robert MacPhail watched his father's face, maybe searching for something of himself. Looking for a sign of the man he'd dreamed about for thirteen years, hounded and chased until he'd finally tracked him down. And what had it been? A few words, a breakfast of bacon and some bitter coffee. He stared at his father and all he could see was that time when Jordan MacPhail had accepted the promise of his mother's money and left him behind without so much as a word. Robert saw that and he saw himself sneaking out on the Apache girl back in San Francisco.

Like father, like son.

Jesus! He hoped not.

Robert walked past his father, past the two wounded gunmen, away down the narrow jetty, gaining on Hart and Fowler with every step he took.